THE WESTERN RAIDER:
THE HAWK RIDES BACK FROM DEATH

THE HAWK RIDES BACK FROM DEATH

By Stone Cody

STEEGER BOOKS • 2020

CHAPTER 1
THE VISION OF BLOOD

THE MAN who knelt before the crucifix set in the rugged crater wall seemed to be looking not at but through it, as though he saw things not there—things far beyond the sheer and jagged surface of the rock.

His eyes burned strangely from the long, upthrusting lines of his narrow, tall-browed face—burned forebodingly, as though he were looking at some unacceptable thing. The tightness about the thin, fanatic mouth was akin to fear.

It was a strange place for a crucifix and a strange man to kneel before it. For if one looked only at the up-wavering lines of the features at once austere and hallowed, it was possible to see in them the countenance of some exalted martyr. But below his face the rawboned, rope-thin body was clothed in a garb not only earthly but verging hellward.

Ivory-handled sixguns, in worn, greased holsters, freighted his lean thighs. Silver conchas, sewn so as to show but not to tinkle, gauded the gold-worked, flaring trousers of a Mexican dandy. A scarlet sash flamed hell-may-care below the rich black silk of a bolero which was also embroidered heavily in gold. The hat held in his hand was no Mexican straw but a specially made, tall-peaked Stetson, of a felt whose fineness spoke not of the piety of heaven, but purely of vanity of this world.

THE HAWK RIDES BACK FROM DEATH

Three men, strolling arm in arm by the kneeling figure, stopped, their wolf-lean faces splitting into understanding grins.

"*Hola, Pablo!*" one of them exclaimed. "What fish do your prayers drag up from the depths today?"

A crash of gunfire blared from the top of the building and the uplifted sword cut a feeble arabesque in the air. Silver moved down off the road.

The suppliant crossed himself, got up slowly from his knees. He turned, and, as he did so, his hand flicked like a lizard's tongue licking. It came out holding the haft of a long-bladed, wicked-looking knife, which glittered in the sunshine.

"Your words blaspheme a little, *amigo*," he said in soft, slurring Spanish, "but your tone even more so. Maybe you will say a prayer of your own, when I have spitted you on this knife, like one of the fish you babble of!"

The man who had spoken did not look impressed, but he released his arm from one of his companions and clasped the hilt of his own knife, which was thrust through his silken sash.

"I have some pesos that say the spitter will be spit, *Pablo mio*," he remarked. "And I think that will be luckier for you than to face the *Jefe,* when he learns that you were first to go for that throat-slitter of yours!"

The long-faced man's expression changed a little. The tension went out of his figure. "It is true that I have forgotten for a moment Silver's prejudice against our fighting," he said grimly. "But do not tempt me too much, friend. Else it may be that they will be burning candles for us both. And for you first!"

"Come, no quarreling, *compadres,*" a second of the strollers cut in hastily. "Miguel, I'm sure, meant nothing by what he said, Pablo. But you did look, old friend, like one who has seen something he would rather not have seen."

Pablo's eyes burned at him. "I have seen disaster, Ricardo," he said, darkly. "If man could avoid his fate, I would beg Silver not to go on this raid he plans."

The man called Miguel threw back his head. He showed his

teeth in a short laugh. "I think you'll have to show Silver more than mere visions, to make him agree to anything like that."

Pablo's face tightened defiantly, as if he were about to utter a heresy. "Silver can make mistakes, also," he said. "On this raid, he will make one that will bring the wings of death brushing us all. Destruction and the scattering of all this crowd is on its way!"

THE MEN stared at Pablo in shocked silence like men who had listened to something impossible to believe. They did not even consider that it might be true, but they were shocked merely at hearing it uttered.

After a moment, all at one time, they turned and looked toward the figure of a man who lay on his back beneath a huge, gnarled cottonwood. Their eyes expressed the feeling almost that they expected this big, lazy-looking figure to rear up and send a lightning bolt of vengeance hurtling toward Pablo, and maybe toward themselves for having listened.

Beside the man under the cottonwood, a girl sat. She was dark-haired, with gentian blue eyes. Her lissome figure breathed grace just in the way she sat. She looked up from the work she was doing with her hands and saw the three men staring in that direction.

"Ricardo and Miguel and Jose look as though they had seen a ghost," she said to the man at her side.

Silver Trent did not stir. His warm gray gaze was fixed on the green of the leaves above him. He said, a little indistinctly through the blade of grass he was chewing, "They have the right to see more than one ghost if they like."

5

The girl's eyes winced a little. Involuntarily, she frowned. "It's still hard for me to—to accept," she murmured.

A shadow darkened Silver's eyes. "Yes," he said softly, "Yes." And then, "This is no life for a girl. I have known that...."

The girl's body moved a little, in a movement like a quick, defensive denial. Her expression changed.

"Don't say that," she said quickly, her voice at once contrite and warm. "I was never so happy as I have been here. It's just hard to realize that sometimes it is necessary to kill men—even though this is a country without real law. But I really do understand, Silver. Don't think me ungrateful or stupid. I haven't forgotten...."

She shivered a little, remembering the insane cruelty on Esteban Varro's face when he had tortured Padre Pete, remembering, too, what he had meant to do to Silver and herself. Except for the cold, reckless courage and panther-like fighting power of this man at her side, except for the fact that he could, and would, kill at need, she would not be here today.

Silver Trent lay very still, his eyes, his whole big body immobile. Even the breath was quiet in his great chest, while he fought down the temptation which clawed at him.

This girl was not for him—an outlaw. He had made himself her guardian. He could do no less, therefore, than guard her against a man who could never offer her a day's peace and security. Against himself....

She had been sitting, sober-faced. Now she raised anxious eyes to his.

"Silver," she said impulsively, "why don't you give up this raid? Why should you ride into danger, risk your life, for a stranger?"

Silver stared broodingly at the backs of his hands. She had asked a question there. His mind flashed back to the time of his friendship with this girl's father—a friendship that had nearly gone on the rocks because of a trivial dispute about water. She had been only five then. Now she was seventeen. Could he make her understand what his life had been since that tragic day when fate had given her into his hands?

"Well," he said, evading a direct answer to her question, "Varro's in it, you know. He and I have some unsettled business."

Unsettled for a longer time than she knew, his thoughts ran on. It had been Esteban Varro who had killed this girl's father. Varro and Phil Cary had been in partnership. Was it greed, Silver wondered suddenly, that had driven the Mexican's murderous hand—or love? Then he knew the answer with a corroding and hateful certainty. It had been greed. Varro had wanted Phil Cary's share of the ranch. His love for Mary Cary, Phil's wife and Gracia's mother had been merely an incident—a kind of lustful greed in itself.

"I wish you could see your eyes!" Gracia's voice came to him at once moved and triumphant. "They look—tragic. You know yourself that this is no life for a man like you. You are too fine for it."

The shadow of an ironic smile tugged at Silver's lips. Too fine to kill? He remembered that day again when he had come to the Cary house to make up his quarrel with Phil. He had found the house in smoke and flame and seen Esteban Varro beat the woman who resisted him into insensibility and then hurl her helpless body into the flaming house. He had seen that from two hundred heartbreaking yards away.

Halfway to the house he had come on Phil Cary's dead body. Even his first racing glance had told him that Phil had been shot in the back. And then he had hammered deadly lead at Esteban Varro. Coldly, with a savage and dreadful anger, he had stood over the Mexican's writhing body and shot him to bloody doll ribbons....

THE GIRL leaned toward the Raider, her eyes pleading. "Oh, Silver," she cried softly, "give it up. I—I...." Her lips were soft, parted. Her breath came a little quickly and along with the plea in her eyes was something else—something Silver dared not recognize.

He remembered now how she had looked, when, terror driving the afternoon sleep from her eyes, she had lain in his arms as he took her out of that burning house.

They had accused him of Phil Cary's murder, and that of Mary Cary and of the fatal wounding of Esteban Varro. Maybe he would have faced those charges if it had not been for Gracia. But if he were hanged for murder who would take care of Phil Cary's girl? He had taken the child and hit for the Border, to be, for the rest of his life, a hunted man.

What could he answer her now? She who had been raised by Padre Pete, knowing nothing of her past.

She didn't even know the reason for the long hate between himself and Esteban Varro, whose master, the Devil, had kept him from dying from those wounds. She didn't know why, recently, Varro had kidnapped her, held her as a bait for Silver.

Silver forced himself to grin teasingly. "To tell the truth," he said, with a slow smile, "I kind of like being an outlaw."

A shadow of disappointment, crossed the girl's face. "Oh, you're hopeless," she said. "But anyway, I'm not giving up. There's no sense in your fighting for this—this Bob Faraday. Suppose he does lose his silver bullion? It's not worth risking lives for. Please! Let it go. I—I've got a feeling that something bad is going to happen."

She had put aside the sixgun she had been cleaning. Now Silver picked it up.

"Looks like I was goin' to need my guns in that case," he said lightly. He examined the Colt with exaggerated care then nodded judicially. "Not bad," he acknowledged. "But do I see a speck of lint there on the outside of the barrel?"

Gracia snatched the gun from him. "No, you do not!" she said, making a face. Then she blew the lint away.

Silver laughed and sat up. The movement of his big body looked lazy, but it was as supple and swift as that of a mountain cat.

"I'm sorry for the rest of the boys not havin' a really good gun-cleaner to make things easy for 'em," he said, by way of reparation.

His gray gaze roamed over the enclosure, taking in the busy cheerfulness of the scene, and his pulses stirred. There were moments when he regretted the sort of life his destiny had forced upon—moments like he had just had, with the pain of his hunger for this girl. But mostly, he had to admit, what he had just said to Gracia was true: he loved it.

This picture of preparation, of cheerful tension, of subdued and smiling eagerness on the part of his crew was old to him, but it never failed to thrill him. These men of his were fighters. Nothing made them quite so happy as the knowledge that they were going to ride again. They moved toward danger as happily as ordinary men went to meet a well-loved mistress.

His eyes warmed to the sight of them—cleaning guns, changing ammunition, grooming horses, mending equipment. Laughter ran in them as brightly as though they had been on their way to a party.

That was what warmed him most. They didn't care that there would be no profit for them. They'd ride thirty miles through darkness to recover a fortune for somebody else, fight, risk death, and ride back no richer than they were before. If there was no loot for them this time, well—there might be some at another time. And anyway, there'd be fun.

Silver grinned suddenly, thinking that the only man in the enclosure who didn't look happy was Bob Faraday. No outlaw, that one. Too much anxiety in him. A nice kid, though. And since it was his bullion at stake, maybe he had a right to look strained.

Silver cast an estimating glance at the sun and got up. Time to really get ready. They had to make an early start if they were to reach the camping place of Varro's under-cover bandits before dawn. Silver knew the trail they would have to take, thought he knew exactly where they would sleep that night. If not…. He shrugged. They might be attacked somewhere on the trail….

The sun dipped suddenly below the rim of the canyon walls and quick, cool shadows ran over the camp.

Pablo, walking moodily toward Silver, shivered. By his side, Miguel grinned. "Somethin' cross your grave, Pablo?"

Silver shot an alert glance at his lean-faced lieutenant. "What's on your mind, old friend?" he asked.

Pablo stared at him. His eyes were still haunted. "This is not a lucky raid, Silver," he muttered. "I feel it. Something is going to happen."

"Let's hope it'll happen to El Diablo and his coyotes, then," Silver smiled at him.

"Would I feel fear in my bones if it was going to be that way?" Pablo asked, half under his breath.

Silver clapped him on the shoulder. "Maybe you've been working too hard, old Pablo," he said. "Why not stay and keep the camp, just this once. I need—"

Pablo wrenched away from his hand and swung to face him. His eyes showed the hurt fury of a child. "Is that what you think of me?" he blazed, "Me—Pablo?"

Silver Trent threw up his hands. "Forget it, old friend," he said. "We ride at dusk, and you with us. What could I do without my good right hand?"

CHAPTER 2
THE PIT OF BLACKNESS

D AWN. THE gray light brightened to reveal a tumbled country of ravines and brush-covered hillsides that ran down into a narrow valley which was itself no more than a major ravine.

Silver eased his horse through a thick growth of scrub oak and into the head of a gully at the top of the ridge. Halted there, his black hat no more than a shadow against the gray dark, he had a straight look into the valley below.

His heart jumped and raced a little, as a hunter's does at sight of quarry. His solid lips flattened and lengthened and a rash, triumphant eagerness sparkled in his gray eyes. There they were! Like bunched cattle, heedless of the wolf pack that stalked them upwind, they were starting to head up the valley. Even in the deeper shadows of the trough, he could make out the mules, already packed for the day's travel, the sacks of gold bullion heavy on their backs. Some of the escort was already mounted, others were still moving about on foot, breaking camp. There were not more than a dozen of men, which made things easy. They could be taken without killing, probably.

The corners of Silver's lips tightened at that thought and his eyes narrowed, suddenly hard and unforgiving. These were Esteban Varro's jackals he was about to attack, and death was too good for them. No man worked for El Diablo who was unwilling to try his hand at murder, or who was squeamish about what happened to the Devil's victims. Varro's path through this

12

world was a swath of killings, brutal robbery, torture, treachery and oppression. These Mexican border-lands would not smile back at the sun until Varro had been sent back to the hell which had bred him.

But Varro was not there among the men. Narrowed, questing, Silver's eyes searched for that hunched, twisted, black-garbed figure, with its long, powerful arms and the thin, dark, infinitely cruel face that was set, almost reckless, between the bull-like, misshapen shoulders.

No sign of Esteban Varro! That was a little strange, for Silver knew the man's immense greed. He should be here, watching over the treasure himself.

Beside Silver, a horse moved up quietly. Pablo's low-pitched murmur reached his ears. *"Jefe,* I smell something evil in this place. Give this raid up. I tell you I have a feeling—"

Silver cut him off with an impatient gesture, then softened it with a quick smile. "You're nervous, old friend. This is a set-up. Let's go to it."

He signaled to the men behind him and moved forward, undercover, following the soft dirt of the gully. In single file his men followed, silent shadow after silent shadow, like gray wolves prowling to the kill.

From below, the sounds of voices and stomping, impatient horses drifted up to them through a silence which had begun to bear insensibly on Silver's nerves. The pocket in the hills was somehow too quiet. No bird-call lifted on the morning air. There was no furtive stir of animals in the brush.

Silver shook himself impatiently. Pablo was making an old

woman of him. The presence of the men down below and the fact that he and his gang were riding down this gully was explanation enough for the silence. Varro's men might be unaware of the raiders, but the keen senses of the animals would have detected them half a mile away.

Behind him, Magpie Myers murmured, "Silver, wait."

Silver pulled up impatiently. The oldster drew alongside, and stood in the saddle, peering over a turn in the gully's bank a little below. His wrinkled old face was enormously alert, his nose quivering, as though it flared the breeze for danger.

"Somethin' moved over in the woods, just the other side of the valley," he whispered. "We ought to watch for a trap here."

Something like anger stirred in Silver. That was the way it went: let one man get nervous and the rest of the gang spooked up like a lot of cattle getting ready to stampede.

"Listen," he said shortly, "that's Varro's gang down there, with about twenty thousand dollars in silver bullion. I'm not lettin' 'em get away with it. Any of you fellows that don't feel like taking a chance can back up. I'm goin' ahead."

He rode on. Magpie, flushed and angry, rode behind him.

THE GULLY gave them full cover until they were within less than a hundred feet of the pack train. At its end, Silver pulled up, looking behind him, to see that the crowd was ready. In that moment of pause, the tug of his instinct for danger was suddenly strong.

He hesitated, wavering on the edge of calling the whole thing off until some other time. Then his mouth tightened and his jaw set. He raised his hand, swung it forward, and jumped his horse

14

Lead snarled around Silver, plucked at his clothing, tore at his
hat. Yelling for the kill, they converged on him.

out of the gully. His hands flashed at the same moment toward his holstered guns.

His horse plunged into the open, covered half the distance to the train in half a dozen lunging strides. Behind him, the gang filed out at the run and spread out behind him, sweeping onward. The men of the pack train were scrambling for cover— any cover.

"Stand in your tracks," Silver's great voice boomed out. "There's enough of us to wipe you out. Throw down your guns and reach for air. The first man that shoots will start a slaughter!"

Then it came, not one gunshot, nor two or three, but a withering blast of concentrated fire! From the trees on the other side of the train. From the brush to right and left. From the very slope down which Silver and his men had just filed!

A sledge hammer slammed Silver in the side, twisted him in the saddle. Shock drained the strength from his great cat-body. Shock double-distilled, because he realized he had led his men into a death trap.

Yet the first hell's tattoo of that fusillade set his chilled brain to racing like a mountain torrent. To attempt to go back along that gully, single file, with the men on the slope there to cut them down, would be suicide. Their only chance was to slam straight through, into the trees beyond the pack train.

"To me! Follow me!" he yelled, and stung his horse with steel.

His guns began to hammer, clearing a swath before him. Behind him was a shambles of squealing, screaming horses and cursing, groaning men. Riderless mounts bolted, kicking and bucking. Then, those of his crew who could still ride were thundering after him, answering lead with deadly lead.

Behind Silver, a high, hated voice squalled, "Kill them, you fools. Cut them down!" Silver turned to see Esteban Varro's twisted, black form raise from the underbrush behind. His body swung in the saddle, his left gun blasting a snap shot. El Diablo's high-crowned black hat jumped from his head, and the man himself dived into the bushes like a rabbit.

Beyond the stampeding pack train at the edge of the trees, two of Varro's hidden ambushers got to their feet. Their guns blazed as Silver's horse bore down on them.

One of them slammed earthward with Silver's bullet in his brain, the other, saved by a hammer that clicked on an empty shell, ducked, running for his life. But Trent kneed his horse into a swerve and brained the man with one downward slash of the empty gun. Then he pulled up swinging around.

"Ride! Keep riding straight ahead until you're clear," he yelled to his onrushing men. "I'll follow!"

As they swept by him, a hand cold as death clutched at his stomach. Barely half of them, he saw, had gotten clear. Half, or more than half, lay dead or wounded where that first murderous volley had caught them. It was his fault! His!

"Get 'em, damn you." It was El Diablo's voice screaming. "They're in a bottle neck there. You've got them trapped!"

Silver, stuffing fresh shells into his guns, looked about him, startled. And then he saw the meaning of El Diablo's shout. Half-concealed by the trees, a deep ravine lay to his right. On the left, the hillside sloped up gently for a hundred yards or so and then lifted sheer in a beetling rock cliff. If ravine and cliff met, as they appeared to do, there might be no way out, or only one so narrow and difficult that his men could be slaughtered from behind as they took it.

A sudden panicked despair ran through Silver. He had not only led his men into a trap, but he had taken the worst way out of it! Varro must have counted on this and planned it carefully. That was why he had left a thin place, almost a gap, in his lines, leading into this blind trail. He had outwitted them thoroughly.

A pain like a thrust of red hot irons began to stab through Silver's body, and the gush of blood down his flank weakened him. For an instant, even his heart gave up. Despair, profound and complete, held him in a grip of paralysis.

Then the big shoulders straightened and the lean jaw clamped shut. By God, Varro's pack might come into these woods on the trail of his men, but they would pay dearly for it. He could not stop them, but he could hold them up, give his men a chance.

THE MOMENT of despair and defeat was gone almost before it had begun. In its place, a savage, killing anger boiled up. It drowned the agony of his wound and drove out his weakness. Coldly, his shock-gaunted hawk face bleak and immovable as granite, he thumbed his newly loaded guns.

They were coming now, with a rush. The open space where the stampeded mules had been swarmed with dark-faced, blood-lusting men—a hundred of them at least. Yelling for the kill, they were breaking cover from all sides and converging on the space where Silver sat his horse.

Slowly, with the monotonous crashing regularity of a stamp

mill, his guns began to talk. Gone was his flashing, incredible speed. In its place was a cold and calculated deadliness. Alternately the guns spoke, and each time they spoke a man died in his tracks.

Lead snarled around Silver, howled about him in a mounting, hysterical crescendo. Lead plucked at his clothing, tore the hat from his head, severed the silver-mounted bridle at the cheek strap, ripped the cantle of the saddle. Yet, miraculously, no bullet touched flesh of man or horse.

Unrelenting, his matched sixguns bellowed their measured song of doom. And death walked out of those woods, touching the leaders of that rush with a violent, destroying finger. The charge stopped. The men who had lusted a moment before for blood had their fill of it. Now their one thought was to find cover, for they saw the manner of this demon they faced. Silver wasted no lead on wounds or misses. He offered only the invisible, flesh-tearing thunk of .45 slugs over the heart, that stopped the yell in the throat and sent the victim falling forward on his face, not to move again.

Behind them, Varro's voice raved, cursing them onward, threatening them with vile tortures. But Varro himself did not appear to lead the charge.

As the twelfth shot sounded and the twelfth man died, Silver Trent's iron challenge rang forth: "Come and get it, Varro—you skulking coyote! Show yourself with your gun, and I'll kill you like the mongrel, yapping dog you are!"

As he spoke, his flashing fingers stuffed fresh shells into red-hot cylinders. With his guns silent, the withering hail of lead began anew. It was not so strong though, now. The right flank of the charge was silent.

Then Silver saw why. A group of some twenty-five men were rushing for the trees along the ravine. It was the breach in the dike. In a moment more, others would follow. He swung his horse, and doing that put himself directly into the howling path of a bullet. It took him high, smashing against his shoulder blade. The shock of it shook him loose in the saddle. In the same moment, the beast under him gave a great leap, as though stung, and Silver went off.

He landed with a crash in the brush, spraddled out, his hands still holding his guns. Almost instantly, he staggered to his feet. A crashing through the trees told him that his wounded mount had stampeded.

His left arm felt numb, useless. His knees shook under him. Yet he remembered those men by the ravine. A split second later, he was running through the trees and brush to cut them off.

A yell behind him told that the Varro men in front had seen him go down. In a moment now, they would be after him. But first things were first. That original twenty-five had to be cut off!

He ran with great staggering strides. Some of the weakness left him and his head cleared. A border of brush loomed before him, and he nearly went plunging over the cliff before he caught himself.

To his left, a crackle underfoot told him that the men he sought were coming. He turned, guns ready. When the first crouching, snaking figure showed, he let him come until the man saw him. The Mexican emitted a squawk and threw up his gun to fire. Then Silver killed him.

Behind the first, the woods swarmed with men, and the beat of gunfire began anew. Smoke and flame lanced out at him. Crouching, dangerous as a cornered lobo, Silver smashed lead in reply.

From the direction he had come, other yells and running steps sounded. New lead began to rip through the leaves, smack into the trunks of the trees. Following it came a thunder of racing hoofs and Magpie Myers' high-pitched bubbling yell. They had come back for him!

Silver cursed, maddened. "Back! Back, you fools! You're spoiling everything."

Something smashed his head and seemed to explode in his brain. He staggered, went to his knees. Teeth gritted, half-sobbing, he fought his way to his feet. The world around him was a dark murk, filled with muzzle-flame and dim, wavering forms.

Something dark appeared before him. He triggered, and saw it go down. Another form loomed to his right. Flaming powder burnt his cheek as he whirled, and his hammer clicked on an empty shell. Lunging, all but blind, he swung the gun, felt it crunch on bone.

The force of his lunge carried him forward, so that he tripped on the man he had felled. Brush lashed at him, but it gave to his weight, and his foot went out into nothingness.

Below, through the red haze in his brain, infinite nothingness looked up at him. Desperately, he fought for balance, felt himself going. This then was death! He struggled for one last shout.

"I'm safe! I'm clear! Go back, you fools!" his great lungs bellowed the words with all power. Then he was whirling, dropping. Down. Down. Faster, as his body gathered acceleration.

Through the blood-haze, rocks and brush rushed up at him. Light, blinding, unbelievably brilliant, flamed in his brain, exploded outward. Then from some inner core, darkness rushed in to drown him.

CHAPTER 3
A MESSAGE FOR EL DIABLO

H E WAS somewhere deep, buried below cottony darkness. It seemed strange to Silver that he did not smother. Then he knew the reason. It was because he did not have to breathe.

He tried to move, but the dark cotton held him close, motionless. He tried to make himself breathe, fought to suck air into his lungs. Pain, dim-felt, ripped through him.

Somewhere he knew, there must be light, if he could only get up to it. His eyelids quivered, and he realized they were closed. Color, very faint and reddish green, began to show through the lids. With an effort, he forced them open.

It was light in the room, cool and dim, but clear. Daylight. Above him, beams showed, half-buried in an adobe ceiling. The ceiling had been washed blue and was peeling. Beyond, a short length of whitewashed wall appeared.

His eyelids felt intolerably heavy. They wanted to close and he fought to keep them open. But they fell shut, leaden, anyway. And he drifted back into darkness.

Later, a long time later, it seemed, he woke again. But still he could not move, and once more he slept.

Then a time came when he opened his eyes and knew definitely that he was alive. A wrinkled brown face was bending over him.

"Hullo," he whispered, "Who—who are—you?"

The reply was in Spanish. "Lie still and rest, Señor. It is better that you do not talk. You have been very near to death."

"*Como se llama Usted?*" Silver whispered.

"*Pancho, señor*—Pancho Bautista, the goatherd."

Silver frowned. He did not know this name. "Where am I?"

"In my poor house, Señor," the goatherd said, and added, with the traditional Spanish courtliness, "*your* house, Señor."

He disappeared then, and Silver felt a little like crying because he could not turn his head. He knew suddenly how a baby feels when things vanish inexplicably from his view.

In a short time, however, the old Mexican appeared again. He had a cup in his hand, and held Silver's head up so that he could drink. The movement made his head begin to ache as though hell's hammers had started in it, but the taste and smell of the hot broth was like life going into his stomach and spreading out through his body.

He sighed with contentment when the cup was empty, and the Mexican let his head down gently on the pillow. Silver would have gone to sleep then, only memory tugged at him. He knew he had been through a bad time. He had smothered under something. It must have been in the desert, for he recalled a hell of thirst somewhere, and he remembered pain, and his own voice raving. There had been a fight, hadn't there? A fight with a lot of men and…. Then the thing snapped back into his mind, and he suddenly groaned aloud.

"Your wound hurts you, Señor?" Pancho's voice was anxious.

Silver did not reply. His eyes were closed and he wished suddenly that he had died along with his men. But after awhile, he slept again.

The despair of the next few days was not enough to keep the magnificent vitality in Silver's big body from getting in its work. He got better with a rapidity which astonished Pancho Bautista.

"It is a miracle, Señor," the old goatherd declared, crossing himself.

Silver learned that Pancho had stumbled over him in the ravine. The goatherd had taken him at first for dead. He was down in some thick brush and covered with rubble which had fallen from the foot of the cliff on top of him. It was a miracle, too, that he had not been killed by the fall—not to speak of the wounds, which were worse than any Pancho had ever seen. A smashed shoulder blade, and a bullet through the lower chest. Another bullet wound in the head. But that had been the least of it.

He had lain in the ravine for two days and nights, surely, for Pancho had heard of the great fight, and it was two days later that he found the Señor. How a man could lose that much blood and live—Blessed Virgin!

It was almost as much of a miracle as the great gringo who

was being cared for by his friend, Juan. *Por Dios*—there was a one! Shot in a dozen places, yet he would not die. A great white bull of a man, yellow-haired, with a chest, Señor, like a hogshead of wine. Bigger, even, than the Señor.

"Dios, Señor! You must not sit up! Do you wish to kill yourself. Lie down, in the name of God!"

"Where? He lives, you say? Where?" Silver's eyes were blazing light.

"Si, si! He lives, Señor. Near here?—at Juan's *casa*. Lie down, Señor."

"And the others? What of the others?"

"I know nothing of others. By the Blessed Virgin, the Señor will break my arm! Dios! This strength is not believable. No, Señor—he alone lived. And the Señor himself. Two miracles in one day, it is enough!"

Silver lay back on the pallet, but the light was not all gone from his eyes. From this day, he had something to get well for. Lars! Lars was alive. And he would know the fate of the others. Silver had heard that booming bellow of his in the chorus when the crowd had come charging back after him. Lars could tell whether they had had a chance to escape or not—and whether they had turned back. He must get to Lars.

TWO DAYS later, Silver got up, despite Pancho's horrified protests, and demanded his clothes. The effort of dressing left him weak and shaken, so that he had to lie back and rest.

He lay gathering his strength, pulling it up from deep inside him. Then he got to his feet. "Come, my friend. We go to Juan's and the other Señor Americano."

Juan's hut was three miles away, up hill and down, and before they got there Silver's knees were shaking so that he could barely walk. His heart pounded so that it seemed he would suffocate. Yet it was not all weakness and fatigue. Part of it was hope, and dread. It seemed to him that more than his life depended on what Lars would have to tell him.

The hut sat high on a tall upthrust of rock. Before it, grazing goats lifted curious heads at their approach.

At the door, Silver paused, panting, gathering his courage. Then he stepped in.

A huge gaunt figure sat on a pallet of straw like that from which Silver had just gotten up. He was growling curses and trying feebly to pull on a boot, so that he did not look up at once when Silver appeared in the doorway. His emaciated bony face was wet with sweat from his efforts at the boot.

"Take it easy, old friend," Silver said softly.

Lars looked up, and the boot came on with a yank. "Silver!" His big, high-cheekboned face lighted up. Unsteadily, he got to his feet.

Silver reached him in two strides, and wrung the big man's bony, almost fleshless fingers.

"Sit down, old-timer," he said. "We got lots of time."

Lars grinned at him. "I ban yust goin' to look you up," he said. "You beat me to it. There ban a durn skinny little Mex aroun' har tryin' to keep me in bed."

"Same with me," Silver grinned back. "By God, I never was so glad to see anybody. How're you makin' it? I hear you were shot up plenty bad."

Lars looked aggrieved, and, somehow, faintly astonished. "I never thought a crowd of greasers could do that to me," he said wonderingly.

There was affectionate amusement in Silver's eyes. He knew Lars. The big man never had really believed that anybody could do anything like that to him. In his heart, he had cherished a secret conviction that his huge body was able to absorb any amount of lead—without harm.

Silver drew a long breath. His face was taut as he asked the question whose answer he dreaded.

"What happened to the others?"

But Lars did not know. He shook his head. He thought that all, or most of those who had escaped the first ambush had probably gotten away. When Silver had first ordered them to go ahead and said that he would follow, they had obeyed, and found themselves in what looked at first sight like a blind alley. Then Magpie had discovered what was little more than a goat trail leading up the face of the cliff and had led them up it—fast. For it was plain that if the Varro crowd reached there in time they could pick them off one by one before they could either reach the top or return to the bottom. Then Silver did not appear, and the firing told them what was happening. So they had picked their way back down that trail, to come to his help.

His shout to go back had checked them, and his final assurance that he had gotten clear had sent them back again. Lars and Magpie and Ricardo had fought a rear guard action, to let the others get up the trail again. Lars' horse had been shot under him, and he had become separated from the others. He had picked cover in the path of the oncoming Varro men and held them off until, shot to doll ribbons, he had lost consciousness. His guess was that Magpie and Ricardo had had time to get away—if they had had sense enough to take it.

The Varro people had evidently thought Lars was dead, though somebody had evidently shot him in the back to make sure, for he had a wound that would have penetrated his heart from behind if a rib had not deflected the bullet.

Silver's gaunt face had gone gray and bleak. He sat motionless, so absorbed in the bitter thoughts which ate at his heart that at first he scarcely felt the timid touch on his shoulder, and Juan's voice saying, "Señor."

With an effort, he pulled himself up out of black depths. "Well?" he asked irritably.

"There are riders coming, Señor—four of them."

Lars Johanssen cursed and got to his feet, his sixgun naked in his hand. "By God, I hope this ban Varro's men. I give them back some of their little presents."

The big man's eyes were blazing as he moved towards the door. Silver was on his feet, too, his hand caressing the butt of his holstered gun. But his other hand reached out to check Lars. "Take it easy, amigo," he said softly. "Maybe we'll learn more by listenin' than fightin'."

A SHARP hail in Spanish sounded outside. Then came the voice of Juan, answering.

"Go on out," Silver said swiftly to Pancho. "Talk to them, but say nothing of us."

The old Mexican went out.

28

Silver led Lars aside, so that they stood with their backs to the wall near the door.

"Friends," the voice outside called jovially. "I bring you good news."

"Good news is always welcome, *Caballero*." This was Pancho's voice.

"How would you like to have rich food in your belly, and a pocket full of silver for wine and the girls, eh, old one? Listen well. The tyrants who grind the poor into the dust are about to fall. My master has declared that humble men shall now be free. Will you join us? Will you strike a blow for freedom and for the riches you've been robbed of? We have the men and the guns—and success is sure."

"In what name do you speak, amigo?" Pancho asked.

"In that of Don Esteban Varro—friend of the oppressed! He offers you good pay, a gun and shells with which to kill your enemies, and rich loot when they are dead. What do you say, amigos?"

"I am an old man." Pancho's voice sounded dubious. "My days for fighting are over. But leave me in peace with my poor goats, Señor, and I shall be content."

"That cannot be, old one. Who is not for us, is against us. If you have good sense, you will join us who are sure of victory. Esteban Varro is already chief of this land. It only remains to strike one blow, to send the coyotes who prey on you scurrying for the brush. Better take your chance now. When the revolution is won, you will be better off. Even now, as you know, one strong enemy is dead, and his band wiped out. *El Halcon de la Sierra* rides no more. Nothing, not even that murdering bandit—may his soul burn in Hell—stands between us and our victory."

Silver's lean, high form had stiffened at Varro's name, while he fought the upthrust of his anger. Now, suddenly, his self-control was at an end. He swung out from the wall and into the doorway.

"You lie, dog," he snapped. "I am not so dead as you think. Take that word to the Devil, your master."

Outside, the four riders sat their mounts with jaws lax, and eyes staring as though they had seen a ghost in the sunlight. But their leader's racing mind had already come upon a plan. He sat with a Winchester across his saddle horn. The gaunt figure in the doorway was armed, though his Colt was safely in holster. Surely a man could flick back the hammer of a rifle and swing the barrel half a dozen inches before even the swift Silver Trent could move.

The Mexican's lips jerked, writhing back over bared teeth. His thumb found the hammer of the rifle and the muzzle moved.

Yet before that movement was completed, Silver Trent drew and shot him dead.

To the men who watched, the thing was like a miracle. The shock of it was eloquent in their faces. Silver had not seemed to move. One instant his hand was at his side. The next, it was held at his hip, with death blasting and bucking in it.

An instant after that, the menacing muzzle covered the other three, while their leader swayed in the saddle, and then pitched outward to thud in the dust.

Slowly, fear-shaken, their hands crept up over their heads.

"Señor, w-we have d-done nothing. Do not kill us...."

The other two voices joined that one, babbling, begging mercy. Fear was stark in their eyes.

Silver's lips curled. "Don't be afraid," he said disgustedly, "I need you—for messengers."

He slid the gun back into his holster, and for a moment it seemed he half-hoped that one of these slinking coyotes might be tempted to make a break or a wrong movement. Then his gaunt body straightened and his chin lifted.

"Go back to the dog who sent you here and tell him that he is mistaken," his voice rang out, menacing. "There will be no revolution. Do you understand that? Tell Varro that Silver Trent spares your rotten lives in order to send him that word. Tell him to hunt his hole, instead—for the men of the Hawk will ride again!"

CHAPTER 4
THE HAWK'S RETURN

FOUR LIMP and discouraged men sat about the smoldering ashes of a fire, the smoke of which curled upward to the blackened arch of a small cavern, to disappear there.

One of them, a Mexican, moved painfully, reached for an ember. He held it between a calloused thumb and forefinger, and lighted the brown paper cigarette he had just rolled. He drew a long inhalation of smoke through sullen lips, staring, narrow-eyed into the gray ash covering of the fire.

"What is the use?" he said. "What can we do—four of us, weak from our wounds? If Silver was here...."

31

He shrugged, and the movement brought a grimace of pain that left the end of his sentence in mid-air.

Across the fire, the sere ghost of a man who seemed at this moment ninety, set the gaunt, wrinkled lines of his jaw in a stubborn outthrust.

"If Silver was here, he'd do somethin'," he growled. "An' so me, I'm doin' somethin'. I ain't sittin' here, lettin' that devil git away with it, without tryin' to saw his horns off afore he gits to pull the trick he's plannin'."

Sombre-eyed, a third man, also Mexican, said, "I do not say I am not willing to fight, Magpie—even remembering that Maria and the boy need me to live. But, *por Dios, amigo,* it is as Miguel says. What can we do? He has an army, that Varro. We are but four. It would be throwing away the lives the good God gave us, without helping the others at all. What is the use? Even now they are after us, and we, like wounded coyotes, are holed up here. They may find us, or they may not. But if we stir from this hideout the chance is that we will be shot down before we have ridden ten miles."

The white-mustached, leathery-faced oldster looked at him out of blazing eyes. "I ain't askin' you ner anybody else to come," he snapped. "All I know is that the men I've rode with is in that hellion's hands. You had the word, same as me. He's fixing to take the town of Sangre tomorrer. He won't have no trouble with that, if'n my figgerin' is right. An' when he does take it, our pardners that fell in his hands are goin' to die in the public square, to make a devil's holiday, and to let everybody see what's the end of gents that goes agin Esteban Varro. The' ain't one of them men but what's fit to ride the river with. The' ain't but one but what I've rode shoulder to shoulder with, an' saved their lives an' had mine saved by them. Pablo's there, an' Doc, an' Beau Buchanan an' half a dozen more that all of you know an' called *compadre*. The Hawk's men, all of 'em—even down to Dave Dennison, what's new but played his hand out like a man. If Silver was here, he'd git 'em loose. Well, Silver's dead. But by God, when the rest of the crowd goes, I can go alongside of 'em—an' will!"

The skeleton of a sandy-haired youngster across the fire pressed his lips together and then opened them. "An' Lars is gone, too," Jim Clane ripped out. "I owe this Varro one for him an' another for Silver. By the grace of God, I'll take El Diablo to hell with me before tomorrer's out!"

Carlos Figuero spread his hands in a gesture of resignation. "You will not ride alone, *amigos,*" he said somberly.

Magpie Myer's keen, shrewd old eyes lighted up in their sunken sockets. He turned toward the fourth man. "Then Miguel can stay behind, to hold down this durn cave an' keep the rattlers out of it," he said sardonically. "It's no blame to him. He's young, an' death ain't easy to face when the blood runs hot an' the gals are soft an' willin'."

Miguel's fierce, mustachioed face went suddenly pale. His hand whipped to the knife sheathed in the bedraggled scarf at his waist.

"Are you trying to say that I am a coward, old one?" he flared.

"I wouldn't rightly say that," Magpie purred. "I'm jest sayin' that I know how you feel."

"Know how I feel! How would an ancient bag of bones like

you know what I feel? *Carrao de leche!* Am I one to be left lolling among the women when men go out to fight? *Por Dios, viejo,* what do you know of the hardness of death when you're half dead already? Keep your eyes on Miguel de la Frontera, and learn how a man rides out to die!"

The shadow of a smile tugged at the withered lips under the white, handlebar mustache. "Why then, I guess we'll all be goin'," he said mildly. "Sorry I kind of misunderstood you, Miguel."

He turned his eyes away, to conceal the flicker of amusement in their depths, and changed position slightly. The movement brought a sudden sweat to his forehead and his eyes clouded. "Durn leg don't heal right," he grumbled.

"Tomorrow night it will be better," Miguel remarked, his eyes wicked.

Magpie nodded. "Reckon that's so," he said, unsmiling. "By tomorrer night it won't be worryin' me none at all."

He turned a bleak gaze out to the sere rocks in front of the cave. They lay silent and hot in the late sun. Beyond them, the arid hills stretched, fold on contorted fold, bare of vegetation except for fringes of greasewood and scattered clumps of jackpine. Only the heat waves blurred the gaunt outlines of the knifelike ridges, which seemed to grin at him in sardonic silence, as though they were somehow akin to the buzzards which circled endlessly against the blue, attracted by the scent of still-open wounds.

"Like you said," Magpie murmured after a moment, "if Silver was here, it'd be different. Silver...."

THE HAWK RIDES BACK FROM DEATH

THE GROUP was silent, as though the sound of that name, spoken with bitter regret, had somehow conjured up the presence of the man himself—whom these tough men had loved as few men in the world had been loved.

A boot heel, scuffing rock, laid its sharp, startling sound across the afternoon stillness. The group in the cave stiffened, hands going toward guns.

Magpie Myers bared his frontier .45, pointed to it significantly and shook his head, in warning to the others not to fire. Their safety depended on taking the intruder prisoner without noise. The blast of a shot echoing across the sounding board of these bare ridges might reach a hundred hostile ears.

The scrape of a man walking, careless, yet light-footed, grew louder, came nearer. Then a Stetson showed over the tops of the rocks just in front, was followed by a gaunt, blond-headed face.

Magpie Myers let out his breath in a sudden explosive curse. Across from him, Jim Clane sat paralyzed for one short instant. Then his hoarse cry broke out, "Lars!"

Lars' eyes had begun to glow. "So you got through, you son of a gun!" he got out. "I might have knowed you was too tough to kill."

Then he looked at the rest and grinned. "Silver said you'd be—"

"Silver?" Miguel's explosive cry rang out.

"Silver?" Magpie Myers' spidery, whang-leather figure shot upward, the pain of his broken, half-healed leg forgotten.

Jim Clane and Carlos had come to their feet, too. "Silver!" Jim's emaciated face quivered. "You mean to say that Silver is…."

"Is here." Silver himself had come up behind Lars, and the voice in which he ended the sentence was husky with emotion.

They stood there, staring at him, unable to speak, unable to move. He came toward them—a great gaunt figure, whetted down to skin and bones, yet still with that mountain-cat walk of his, still with the sense of power in the easy play of the iron muscles.

He brought up a few paces from them, his gray eyes warm, yet filled with a deep and bitter sorrow. "And is this all of you?" his deep voice asked gently. "So few? And yet you can look at me without hatred—with eyes that make it needless for me to ask your pardon?"

Magpie Myers looked faintly astonished. "Why, Silver," he croaked, trying to swallow his Adam's apple, "what the hell are you talkin' about?"

But Miguel's fierce face was lighted up with understanding. "He means," he said proudly, "that he led us into a deathtrap—he means that he thinks he is a murderer." He flung back his head and laughed exultantly. "I knew it. I knew that in hell he was thinking of us, his children, and hating himself for the one mistake he ever made. What do you think, *Jefe*, that we are dogs to turn and snap at your heels because you were too brave to be cautious? Do you think there is a man of those who died who is not swaggering in hell and pulling the nose of Satan himself, because he rode to his death at your side?"

Silver's chin had come up. A quiver ran through the lean jaws whose muscles were locked against the emotion that ran in him. Now the gray eyes had begun to blaze.

"You think that?" he asked. "You think that, Miguel?"

Miguel laughed again. "What do you think?" he countered. "What do you think of Ricardo, say? We left him dying, *Jefe*. He fell out of the saddle when we were no more than five miles from that place—a man already dead. He thought you had gone before him. For you were seen to fall over the cliff when you cried that last great lie to us. He would not let us stay with him, for there were a hundred of those devils on our trail, pressing us hard, and he knew that he was done for. Yet with the death in his eyes, he grinned that grin of his—*Madre de Dios!* We will never see its like again—and said to the thing he saw, 'Come on, Old One. Take me. I go with Silver to run the Devil out of Hell!'"

Silver's chin dropped on his chest. When he looked up, pride was clear in his eyes. "And the others? There are no others?"

THE TENSION broke then, and the talk boiled up. They spoke all at once, so that he had to quiet them before he could make sense of what they said.

They had come back for him, as he knew, and Pablo had seen him go over the cliff. The news of it had set a madness loose in the men. Instead of going back, they had charged on, maniacs, filled with a fighting fury which had driven the Varro men before them like trash in a breeze of wind. But that had been for a moment only. The odds against them were too great. One by one they went down, until these four were the only ones left.

Sanity had come back to Magpie then, and under his leadership they had escaped up the cliff path. Wounded, exhausted, they had been driven from hideout to hideout. Varro had never stopped. He had sworn that he would never rest until the last of the gang was dead. Once, a couple of weeks before, they had been nearly trapped, had fought their way out, but not one of them without getting new wounds.

Now the news had come to them that nine of the gang were in Varro's hands. There had been ten, for Bob Faraday had been among them. But, someway, he had managed to escape. The others had been too badly hurt.

El Diablo, out of sheer cruelty, had treated them as though they had been his own brothers. He had sent a hundred and fifty miles for the best physician in the countryside, to save their lives—for another death he planned for them!

It was thought at first that El Diablo meant to torture them slowly, but only yesterday the news had come that he had another plan. He was beginning his revolution by taking the town of Sangre, and he had announced everywhere that Silver's men would be executed in the public square after the town was taken, as a warning of what happened to men who resisted Varro.

The event would mark the death of his greatest enemies, and the beginning of his greatest triumph. For no one doubted that Esteban Varro would win the revolution. He had collected an army of four or five thousand men, most of them well armed. The Federal troops were not numerous enough to put up a real fight against him, and his name inspired such terror in the countryside that no one could be recruited to take arms against him.

Silver listened, with the glow of excitement deepening in his eyes.

"Nine of them," he said at last. "And Pablo and Doc and Beau among them! That makes fifteen of us in all. It's enough!

Padre Pete

Silver Trent

Gracia

It's enough for a beginning. What happened to the men at the hideout?"

"Still there," Magpie told him. "Varro found out where it was, all right, but he couldn't take it. So he's got it blocked off, figgerin' to see that we couldn't get in nor the others get out."

"Then that's nineteen!" Silver slapped his thigh.

Magpie grinned. "Twenty, if you count Big Nose Beaujolais. We hear tell that he had a leg shot durn near off, but managed to git into some bushes before he passed out. Then, when he come to again, he crawled fourteen miles before anybody found him. A couple of freighters picked him up an' took him up to the Dorado Mine, where the company sawbones took his leg off, above the knee. They say the Canuck got up off the table they had laid him on an' tried to kill the doc when he found out they was fixin' to chop his leg. But they got him down an' done it anyways, gangrene havin' set in an' there bein' no other way out of it. They didn't have no chloroform an' Big Nose yelled that he'd like to see the gangrene that was meaner'n what he was."

Silver chuckled. "We'll put him on permanent duty at the hideout."

He got to his feet, looking like a new man. "We'll ride tonight," his voice crackled. "Lars, go out an' bring in the horses. We brought you some grub, boys, thinking that you might be shy of it."

"How'd you hit our trail?" Jim Clane asked wonderingly.

Magpie gave him a glance of disgust. "Hell, son," he boasted, "what Silver didn't know about sign, I taught him. That's how he hit it."

Silver laughed. "It was a pretty cold trail, Jim," he winked, "but there was still some sign left, an' then, the buzzards were circling high, so Lars an' I figured there was somethin' aroun' here too tough for 'em to digest. It wasn't hard to guess that was Magpie."

Laughter ran around the circle. Discouragement had gone

out, its place taken by an electric current of new hope. Nobody asked how six men were going to rescue nine prisoners from an army. They were content to leave that to Silver Trent. It was enough that he was back with them.

And then, in the distance, a Winchester laid its thin, wicked report across the late afternoon air, and a bullet slapped into the rocks above the cave. An instant later, Lars was climbing up the rocks, dragging saddlebags and cursing savagely.

"Varro men!" he ripped out. "They must have spotted me while I was leading the horses. There's a couple of dozen of 'em, comin' fast!"

CHAPTER 5
LAST STAND

DAYBREAK LAID a pall of silence over the town of Sangre. As the shadows lightened, the streets showed full of quiet movement, but there was little talk. From time to time, the face of a woman, pallid and anxious in the gray light, showed at a door or a window, to murmur a question to some passerby, and to receive a toneless answer. But apart from that, the ordinary human sounds were strangely lacking. Sangre was like a town stricken by the plague.

At the western edge, a rough barricade had been thrown up. Behind it was a company of soldiers in the ragged, nondescript uniforms of the Federal army. To the right and left of them was a collection of grim-faced citizens, some two score in all, armed with all manner of weapons, shotguns, old-fashioned single-shot rifles, new Winchesters, ancient revolvers, machetes, even pitchforks.

Behind these, like a general, paced a stocky, bandy-legged man in a priest's cassock, the fringe of white hair about his bald head showing like a cloudy halo. The cassock was caught up at the sides, to give greater freedom of movement to the bowed, strongly muscled legs. One of his hands rested on a crucifix which hung from his neck, and his lips moved faintly, as though in prayer.

Behind him, at some distance, a crowd of the curious stood. With fear-haunted eyes and nervous glances they looked out over the plain ahead, to where, in the growing light, movement showed in a long line where El Diablo's army formed.

A figure emerged wearily from the street and ran toward the priest. "Padre Pedro," he said, panting, hat in hand, "I have tried everywhere but there is no one else who will fight. All men say the thing is…."

He stopped suddenly, embarrassed.

"Madness?" the priest supplied gently. "Do not be afraid of the truth, my son."

The peon spread his hands. "It is only what *they* say, Padre," he acknowledged.

"Madness," Padre Pete muttered. "So it may be. And yet, we face only death, which comes in the end to all. Is it not better that we go to the good God saying, 'We have fought against evil', rather than 'we have bowed the neck to the Devil's work in fear of our miserable hides?' No! If the cause be hopeless, then so much the more our virtue, my son. Go take your place—if you will—in the fighting lines."

From the gray plain ahead, a bugle sounded, and the long line of Varro's men began to move forward.

Padre Pete moved along behind the slender forces he had gathered. "Hold your fire, men," he said quietly. "We have no ammunition to waste."

He shot a glance at the commander of the *Federalistas*, who was looking nervously over his shoulder toward the buildings of the town. He frowned a little.

A peon girl, shawled, barefooted, garbed in a shabby black dress, came toward the priest. "Padre," she cried, "Padre. I feared this. Have you no wisdom to be trying something like this?"

For an instant, the priest stared uncomprehendingly at her face, stained brown as an Indian's, then he gasped. "Gracia! Daughter, daughter! Have you lost your mind? What are you doing here?"

The girl smiled faintly. Seen close, she was recognizable as the slender girl who had cleaned Silver Trent's gun for him, and shuddered despite herself at the thought of killing. Only now, the great, dark-blue eyes were hollowed and shadowed by grief and anxiety and the soft mouth was set in lines of enduring sadness.

"Did you think I would stay in safety and let the man I love die alone?" she asked.

Padre Pete wrung his hands. "You must go back," he cried hoarsely. "Child, have you forgotten what it will mean if Esteban Varro sees you. Go quickly. Hide. And when this is over, get back to the hideout as quickly as you can."

Gracia's mouth pulled into a half-smile. "It was not worth much, living without Silver," she said. "It will be nothing now. No. I will take the gun of the first man who falls, and do my share toward fighting this Devil. And if I live to fall into his hands, then I promise you that he himself will die before many days are out. I am not a woman for nothing. I think I have charms that will soften him, a little—long enough…."

The priest's eyes were suddenly compassionate. "You loved him—Silver—did you not, my daughter?"

"As a woman loves," the girl answered simply.

Padre Pete sighed. "Aye, we all loved him. Yet you—I had hoped it was a love like ours—not that love which tears the heart and burns like a consuming flame in the very flesh itself."

The girl looked at him in sudden wonder, through the tears that had sprung into her eyes.

"You—you speak almost as though you had known what it is to love, Padre," she murmured.

The priest smiled gently, the round, jolly look of his face relaxing into lines of an old sadness. "Even I once was young and—not a priest," he said.

A WINCHESTER cracked suddenly from the line of men in front of the priest. Out on the plain, a solitary figure threw up his hands suddenly, his rifle arcing outward. Then he plunged face forward to the ground.

Instantly, an answering fusillade rippled down the long

Varro line. Lead hummed and snarled in the air overhead, or bit viciously in the improvised barricade.

"It's no use. Give way! To the rear, march!"

It was the commander of the *Federalistas* who yawped that order, his voice suddenly high and urgent.

The response was instant. His troops swung away from the barricade and began a retreat into the town.

Padre Pete stared after them, his mouth open a little. "I feared that these men would not stand well," he breathed after a stunned moment, "but this—without a single shot!"

Gracia laughed briefly. "Varro bought them. The word is being whispered everywhere. They were afraid he might not win in the end, so they dared not go over to him openly. But this way, they will be both safe and—rewarded."

Her low-pitched, vibrant voice was suddenly harsh with contempt.

Padre Pete's face flushed with honest anger. He strode over to his men.

"This makes it really hopeless, my sons," he called out. "It would be better for you to throw down your weapons and hide now. It is a choice for you to make—to fight vainly, or run. I can no longer ask you to sacrifice yourselves."

A lean-jawed Mexican, with bitter eyes, laughed carelessly.

"There are only some five hundred of them, Padre," he called. "This Varro is a liar as well as a thief. Where are his thousands? For me, I will handle this half a thousand alone, with a skinning knife."

Reckless laughter ran along the line.

"Are we rabbits, to run when the coyotes bark?" a stocky, scar-faced man yelled.

"These are dogs that fight because their bellies are empty. We'll serve them with lead and see how they like it to be full-fed," a savage-eyed ruffian chimed in.

The shout of approval which followed left no doubt as to the sentiments of the others.

Padre Pete seemed to swell in size. "Ah!" he cried. "Ah! But you are such men as Silver Trent might have loved! You are fit to have hunted with the Hawk! May the Saints bless you and make your aim true."

For a moment there was silence while these men stared at him—a silence so long that he wondered if he had said the wrong thing to them. Then the sudden flame that swept along their faces told him he had chosen the compliment above all others with which to touch their pride and lift their courage. With a wild yell, they turned back to the barricade.

The firing from in front had ceased after the retreat of the *Federalistas*. The priest guessed that Varro wished to make this a bloodless victory, for the sake of his prestige. But now, as guns began to crack from behind the barricade, the storm of lead from the attackers began again, doubled in intensity.

Its very volume was overwhelming, even though it lacked accuracy. These men in front, with their new repeating rifles were, for the most part, deluded peons who had been pressed into service through fear and their own greed. A quarter their number of well-armed and trained men could have checked and driven back that advance in short order. But the odds were not

46

four to one; they were two score to one, and the defenders were not even well armed.

Padre Pete guessed that nothing could save his crowd from annihilation, and his conscience was gravely troubled at taking them all with him to death.

AT THE barricade, a man flung up his arms and staggered backward, dropping his rifle. Padre Pete's lips tightened and a look of pain was in his eyes as he went forward. The man had been hit badly, he knew. But before he had taken a step, a slender figure flashed out from his side and darted to the barricade.

For an instant, Gracia knelt by the side of the fallen man, and her hand went to his forehead as she murmured some word. Then she snatched up the Winchester from the dust at his side, and moved swiftly into his place, snapping the rifle to her shoulder.

Padre Pete groaned a little, but, wisely, he did not attempt to interfere. When he knelt by the side of the wounded defender, he saw that he was shot through the lungs and would die quickly. His eyes were closed as though he were already unconscious.

Hastily, the priest administered the last rites. When the final, solemn word had been murmured, the man opened his eyes, and the Padre saw that they were filled with a strange ecstatic light.

"*Gracias, Padre,*" the man gasped, a smile on his lips. "But I think—I—have already been—touched by—an angel." Then the blood came into his mouth and his head fell sideways, but the smile was still on his lips.

Padre Pete looked up at the girl's back, his eyes misted. "God sometimes bestows his blessings in other ways than through the Church," he muttered.

He stood up, his glance running down the line of defenders, oblivious of the constant scream of lead about his ears. One man had ceased firing to fix his neckerchief into a sling for a smashed arm. Another was down. The priest was about to go to him when a sudden sortie from the street caught his attention.

A scare-crow party of half a dozen peons, bare-footed, ragged, but armed with business-like looking Winchesters, and the crossed Mexican cartridge-belts, was coming on the run toward the barricade. The man in the lead, a gaunt, sun-blackened figure, ran with a limp and held one shoulder higher than the other. The posture made him look awkward, but there was, somehow, in this cripple, a feline grace that touched a chord in Padre Pete's memory. Behind him ran a huge skeleton of a man, bigger than any Mexican the priest had ever seen—bigger than he ever believed a Mexican could be.

So much his first glance told him. Then Padre Pete stiffened, and his breath caught in his throat. That gaunt man in the lead, he of the catlike grace, if it had been possible he would have believed…. But no, that man was surely dead. Only….

The priest held himself motionless, hardly daring to breathe. Then, as the group came closer, the clear light of morning showed him a hawk-like, powerful face out of which blazed a pair of luminous gray eyes.

"Silver!" The padre's voice was a broken cry of joy. "Silver! *Hijo mio!*"

At his side, a man whirled away from the barricade, staring. *"Que? Que dice Usted?"* he demanded sharply.

Others nearby had turned.

But the Padre was unaware. Tears were streaming down his ruddy cheeks as he walked toward Silver, his hands held out. *"Hijo mio! Hijo mio!* What miracle is this, my son?"

"I'm hard to kill, eh, Padre?" Silver's own voice was husky as his hands found those of the priest. "But we'll talk later, shall we? Looks as though you had a fight on your hands here."

"Yes, yes!" Padre Pete sounded beside himself with excitement. He whirled, calling, "Men! Do you know who this is? *El Halcon de la Sierra*—not dead, but alive and here! Silver Trent! God has sent him back to us in our time of need."

At the barricade, the firing had ceased. The men were staring, as though unable to believe their eyes and ears. Then a wild shout went up. The sound of it, savage and triumphant, stilled the attackers' fire, halted them momentarily, struck with wonder.

Silver's glance sparkled down the line. "We're proud to get here in time to fight by the side of *men,*" he said. "But remember, don't call my name. I'm in disguise because it will be better if friend Varro does not yet suspect that I am here. And now, let's get at it."

The gesture of his arm swung them to their posts, and sent the five who had come with him to the firing line at the same time.

It was only then that his eyes took in the slender figure which, back to the barricade, had stood staring as though she could not fill her eyes with him. Gracia's face was deathly pale, her eyes at once stunned and glowing.

Silver's glance ripped through her peasant disguise instantly. His lean face flamed with sudden happiness. "Gracia!"

CHAPTER 6
A FALSE ORDER

IT WAS as though the word had waked her from a trance. She ran to him, flung herself into his arms. Her lips found his, clung to them, fiercely, passionately.

The shock of it held Silver rigid for a moment. He had expected affection, even a sister's or a daughter's love from this girl. But there was nothing sisterly in this kiss. It sent a gasping tremor through his big frame, set fire to burning along his veins.

He tried to keep his head, tried to tell himself that now, less than ever, had he the right to the love of a girl like this. But it was useless. The passion he had kept down with an iron hand had its way with him now, swept his defenses aside in one tremendous, overwhelming rush. His arms went around her, crushed her to him. His lips met her kiss, mastered the passionate urgency of her mouth, so that it was as though he had wooed and conquered her, rather than the other way.

There were few to witness that scene, for most of the men were too busy dealing death to the advancing Varro horde to see anything else, but those who did see, recognized it for what it was—a betrothal, the meeting of a man and his mate. And they told it, later—of this troth plighted silently, while enemy lead snarled in the air around them—as a fitting thing, as a warrior's marriage, with the beat of the guns for a wedding march.

It was in fact the pluck of a bullet at the lobe of his ear that roused Silver to the danger the girl was in. She had gone limp in his arms, her soft mouth submissive, and their cheeks were wet with the tears that streamed from between her closed eyelids.

For an instant, Silver's heart turned cold with the fear that she had been hit, while he had held her there. But when he took his mouth from hers, she stirred, and the shine of her eyes looking up at him assured him that it was only happiness which had drained the strength from her.

He smiled at her briefly, then released her gently.

"Down," he said softly. "Get down under cover. You have no business in this."

Then he went swiftly to take her place at the barricade. In an instant she was at his side, her mouth set stubbornly, and her rifle in her hand.

"No use to talk," she told him, with quiet determination. "I'm going to fight at your side. Everyone of us is needed here."

Silver Trent looked at her and tried to say no, but then something grew in him, a pride, an acceptance. From now on, he knew, his dangers must in part be her dangers.

And so quietly, with his jaw a little set, but with a strange tranquility in his eyes, Silver Trent turned and swung the Winchester to his shoulder.

The Varro line showed ragged gaps now, and the advance was so near that the details of the attacker's dress and figures could be clearly seen. Automatically, Silver's mind paid tribute to El Diablo's shrewdness and thoroughness of planning. These peons were in new uniforms, strikingly military enough to appeal to the wearer's pride, yet not too conspicuous against the brown Mexican earth to be impractical. They were magnificently armed and accoutered, with the latest type rifles and packs. Everything, in fact, had been done to make soldiers of them, except length of training and the "blooding" which, by some queer transmutation, turns the polished lead of the trained recruit into the gold of the seasoned fighter.

Trent sighted swiftly, squeezed the trigger and saw, with almost detached interest, the man he had fired at halt in midstride and go down. He knew then that he had estimated the range and the windage rightly, and settled himself to his work.

As he levered, he saw another man drop near the man he himself had downed, and grinned faintly. If his guess about the frontage was right, that would be Magpie's work, for the man had fallen as a man falls who is shot in the head, and the range was close enough now so that Magpie would not be shooting for any other target. "Men," the oldster was wont to say, "is like game. It's best not to shoot 'em unless you have to, but if'n you have to, why then kill, don't cripple."

Then Silver saw that Varro's men had, after all, received some training. The real advance was beginning now. A bugle sang a shrill, repeated note, and the long line dropped, fixing bayonets. Then, at another signal, they moved forward again, this time by rushes of squads. While one squad tore forward, it was covered by rapid fire from those who stayed behind. After that, the rear squads moved up, themselves covered by fire from the first.

SILVER FED new shells into his hot gun and increased the tempo of his firing. The movement of his right hand as it levered the Winchester was a swift blur. His eye notched the front sight in the split second during which the steady pressure of his finger tripped the trigger. And in less than five seconds, five men died.

Beside him, slower, but with a steadiness which sent a thrill of pride to his heart, Gracia's Winchester beat a steady counterpoint to his own.

Then, refilling his magazine, he tensed. The rear squads, this time, had moved up level with the front squads. The charge proper was about to begin. An instant later, the wild, urgent sound of the bugle rang out. The line leaped to its feet and surged forward, not firing, but running in silence.

"Break it—break it!" Silver's great voice shouted. "Shoot fast and don't miss."

In response, a sudden storm of deadly fire broke out from the barricade. Gaps showed, swift and ragged, in the advancing line. At the center, a man faltered, unhurt, but a victim of fear. Beside him another halted. Beside him a third dived for the cover of some nearby brush.

The charge wavered, halted, gave back. A yell of unbelieving triumph went up from the barricade. The unbelievable had happened. Some thirty men, half of them badly armed, had stopped the advance of half a thousand!

Silver laughed, thinking of what Esteban Varro must be feeling, yet knowing, too, that this was far from the end, and that the end, as far as this fight went, was hopeless.

He looked down the line of the barricade. Half a dozen men were down. As many more were more or less badly wounded. Yet, as though they had some magic protection, not one of his own men was hit. He saw Lars Johanssen, upright and careless, evidently wholly unimpressed by the lesson he had had: that bullets really could hurt him. Jim Clane with his eyes blazing, not interrupting the work of his gun to cheer, but sighting carefully at a head that showed above a fold in the ground. Miguel, his lips parted in a laugh of contempt. Magpie, calm-faced and shrewd-eyed, squatted behind the shelter of the barricade, stuffing shells into his carbine. Carlos Figuero, his face fired by the lust of battle, squeezing trigger in a final shot.

Then, in the distance behind the enemy lines, a group of horsemen got into motion. Three men, riding at full gallop, bore down on the center of the halted line. The others circled, racing toward the flank.

Instantly, Silver comprehended the maneuver. Varro meant now to attack at both flanks at the front. He would send a detachment of infantry to the left. The mounted men would attack on the right. The remainder would drive forward again. It was what he should have done in the first place, and would have done, Silver guessed, had he not been so confident that the retreat of the Federal troops would kill all effective resistance. Varro must be raging now at this check to his triumphant entrance into the town. Then Silver saw that Varro was, in fact, in a fury, for he was riding at the head of his own cavalry!

Not that Esteban Varro was a physical coward. Silver had no illusions about that. It was simply that he was possessed of an arrogance, a cynicism and a cold selfishness so profound that he never took an unnecessary risk. He paid out good money to have his fighting done for him, and only an emergency, or a complete loss of temper, could put him at the head of his men.

These thoughts flashed through Silver's mind during the instant he was raising his rifle for a shot at one of the three riders who were driving for the center of the line. These men, he knew, were messengers, carrying Varro's orders. If they could be stopped, the maneuver would be delayed or would go wrong. He shot once, missed, levered fast and shot again.

The man he had under his sights left the saddle as though the bullet had knocked him over backwards. In the same instant, Magpie's rifle cracked and a second rider plunged sideways to the ground. His foot caught in the stirrup and his stampeding horse dragged him.

But the third man got there, quit the saddle on the run and took cover.

A moment later, a detachment at the end of the line began to move outward, in the flanking movement Silver had anticipated.

Silver smiled down at Gracia, who was reloading her rifle. "Time to move," he said cheerfully.

Then he called down the line, "Move back to the street, boys—on the double!"

There was a moment of hesitation. These undisciplined fighters were filled with the lust of battle and the flush of triumph. They didn't want to give way. Yet, a moment later, they were trotting back toward the street, having found, as so many others had found before them, that there was a quality in Silver Trent which got his commands obeyed without any need of repeating them.

Varro's circling riders had swung in along the town's edge

now, driving straight for the flank of the barricade. A savage yell went up from their throats as they saw the defenders retreating. IT WAS a yell that changed to shouts of dismay when the first blasting volley hit them. For Silver had chosen his spot swiftly and well. The sides of the street here were uneven, one house protruding beyond the end. This house formed a rear-wall which protected the backs of the defenders from the flanking infantry detachment. And the end of its yard was marked by a board fence which gave cover from the infantry which was now charging from in front of the barricade.

Yet since the lot across the street was vacant, Silver's men had a clear field of fire toward the advancing horsemen.

Instantly, what had been a charge, became a broken, milling pandemonium. Exploding gunfire mingled with yells of pain and anger, and the scream of wounded horses. That first withering volley had emptied the lead saddles or downed the lead horses, so that the riders behind piled up on top, in a confused and deadly tangle.

It was the turn of the defenders to set up a fierce shout of triumph, but Silver Trent cursed bitterly. He had had his sights lined on Esteban Varro, and had missed his kill because something in him delayed his trigger finger a fraction of a second too long. This was not the way he wanted to kill Varro. He wanted to face him single-handed and give him full chance for his rotten life. Yet, he knew that now was a heaven-sent chance to end this revolution and rid the world of a fiend who would bring it nothing but murder, oppression and evil. And so he pulled the trigger anyway. But in the instant he had hesitated, a bullet took

Varro's horse squarely in the forehead. Horse and man plunged earthward just in time to make Silver miss.

Varro's black-clad, vulture-like form hit the ground rolling, and was at once covered by the cloud of dust which swirled as the charge piled up. It was impossible to see what had happened to him, but Silver had the impression that he had rolled clear and was unhurt.

He levered and began pouring lead into the milling mass of the broken charge, as his men were doing. It was a trap, a slaughter. No troops could have stood against it.

At the rear of the riding dust cloud, a rider whirled his horse and spurred away, leaning low in his saddle and riding as though the devil were after him. Another followed and another. Varro's squawling, cursing voice lifted to check them, but it did no good. Every man who could still ride turned and fled.

At the sound of that voice, Silver stopped firing, his narrowed eyes trying to pierce the dust cloud. But Varro, it was evident, had found cover. He was not in sight.

The defenders now were shouting taunts and catcalls, daring the enemy to come on.

"Back! Down the street!" Silver commanded brusquely.

They looked at him, open-mouthed, as though he had betrayed them. But Silver knew that the attackers were even now vaulting the barricade and that the flanking detachment would be coming up in the rear. It would not take long for them to figure that the thing to do was to cut through the back yard of the house behind.

He grinned at his men. "Come on, you fighting hellions," he called. "Don't be afraid that I won't give you plenty of action!"

And again they obeyed him, reluctantly.

It was just in time. The first of the attackers poked a rifle around the corner of the board fence before they had backed up twenty yards, and a few moments later men began to swarm through the backyards on the right.

It was a slashing, savage retreat, with Silver's men running, taking cover in every alleyway and behind every fence, yet keeping together and smashing so deadly a fire down the street as to keep the overwhelming force of the enemy constantly in check.

It was also a series of narrow escapes. For Varro had reassembled his riders, and they, too, were attempting to cut the defenders off from the side and rear.

But Silver's expert timing avoided that. He brought his group through, with remarkably few casualties, to Padre Pete's high-walled house.

The last short dash to the house led them through an alley where they were out of sight of the attackers. Silver assembled his men rapidly and said, "Pay no attention to what I'm going to say." Then he bellowed in Spanish. "We can't win. Separate! Scatter! Get rid of your guns and get into hiding. Hurry...."

It was after that that they raced, as a group, to the Padre's house.

In the street beyond, the Varro men, hearing this cry, shouted and came swarming. For a few moments, there was an undisciplined man-hunt in progress which was stopped shortly by Varro's orders.

"Get your men together," he snapped to the colonel in command of the attacking force. "Let these fools go, for the moment. We'll send squads later to rout them out. Right now, I want the column to march into the town, in order, to show the people we've won. Meanwhile, throw a cordon around the outskirts and see that nobody leaves. Later, when we've had the execution, we'll round up these fools that fought us!"

CHAPTER 7
THE HAWK RIDES AGAIN!

MINUTES LATER, the triumphal parade began. It took place through a town that had a curious undertone of silence. There was cheering along the way, but the quality of enthusiasm was lacking, and the voices were purely male. No woman showed her face at door or window.

Varro, riding at the center of his column, scowled, his thin lips setting in a cruel line. Anyone who knew him might have guessed that he was considering turning his wolves loose on the town itself.

Behind him, marched his prisoners, their wrists bound behind their backs. They were tied together, also, by a rope which encircled their necks, and made it necessary for them to march in single file. A double line of soldiers guarded them closely on either hand, and behind them rode mounted men, to run them down in the practically impossible event that any should get loose.

The men of the town, thinly lining the walks and lifting

59

their forced and nervous cheers, stared at the prisoners, open-mouthed, as they passed. They had seen them before, most of them. They had seen them ride, fierce and proud and high-headed, through the streets of this same town not many days before Federal soldiery, after having rescued certain Americanos from a firing squad.

It was strange to see them now, tied together like cattle, marched afoot like peons, to face a firing squad themselves, And yet, they walked high-headed and fierce still. No pallor, other than that of long illness whitened their faces. No tremor shook those hard lips, and no trace of fear showed in the hard, scornful glances of their eyes. Beside the shambling, barefooted peons who guarded them, pretentious in their new, ill-fitting Varro uniforms, they looked like wolves stalking proudly in the midst of slinking and mangy curs.

The sudden quiet that greeted their presence augmented that queer undertone of silence which had persisted even beneath the cheering. Instead of adding to El Diablo's triumph, these nine, fierce-eyed men bade fair to spoiling it entirely.

"*Mira!*" the whispered recognition ran, "It is Pablo, the Pious, who fears not man nor devil, but only God and his Holy Saints."

"And behind him the big doctor with the name from Hell."

"Aye! The name from Hell but not the man, *amigo.* When my cousin fell sick of the yellow sickness, it was he who…."

"Look! Behind him—is it not the gambler who—? *Por Dios,* he is dressed like one who goes to a *baile!*"

So the whispers ran, not in mere curiosity, but with admiration in them and regret. For these were the men of the Hawk, and no one of the honest poor had suffered anything from them, other than kindness and sudden, dazzling largesse, in their moments of need. These were the men of the Hawk, who took from the rich and gave to the poor, whose swift, high justice was known both north and south of the Border; who had courted danger like a mistress, but whose hands had been readier to succor the oppressed than to fill themselves with rich loot. These were the men of the Hawk…. But the great *Halcon* himself was gone, and now these, too, walked without fear to look on the face of Death.

Little wonder that the strained cheers fell silent, and mute sorrow shadowed the watching eyes as the mutter ran: *"Ay de mi! Que pena!* Better that the Devil and all his ways be sent back to Hell than that these should die."

After hearing that mutter, catching its quality, El Diablo's face darkened with fury. Mutely, he turned and stared back at the nine, the hatred in his eyes showing frustration and venom.

"Por Dios," he said under his breath, "I have made a mistake. It would have been better for me to give myself the pleasure of killing them slowly." But it was too late for that. He had announced the public execution of the last of the men who had dared oppose him, and now he must go through with it.

The procession turned into the square. A series of curt orders put the troops in a three-sided rectangle, the fourth side of which was formed by the blank wall of a building. Against this wall the prisoners were lined up, the rope still about their necks. BEHIND THE troops, pressing in, drawn by a morbid fascination, most of the population of the town had gathered.

Into the center of the square formed by the troops and the blank wall before which the prisoners stood, Esteban Varro rode, magnificent on a black stallion which had been brought up for him when the horse he rode had been shot under him. He held up his hand for silence, then spoke.

"My friends," his voice rang out, "you have seen today the first triumph of the forces of liberty. You have been oppressed. You have been made poor, and ground under the heel of your rulers. Through me, and through these brave men who have fought for you, you shall be set free. From now on, I, Esteban Varro, shall be your ruler and your father.

"In token of that, and in token of the defeat of the forces of evil, I give you here today the death of nine scoundrels. They are all that is left of the band of thieves, murderers and marauders who served under the outlaw called Silver Trent. Silver Trent is dead, killed by my own hand. These, the last of his gang, shall die now—as a warning to anyone who in the future may be so foolish as to oppose and defy the power of Esteban Varro."

He wheeled his horse and rode to the far side of the square, sitting with his back to the crowd, in apparently magnificent carelessness of the possibility that someone would shoot him in the back. Yet the observant may have noticed that in addition to the rifles of the soldiers, the rear rank of whom was turned facing the crowd, he was immediately joined by other riders, who sat their horses facing outward around him.

Among these riders were three who exchanged significant and uneasy looks. They might have told Esteban Varro that the man he spoke of so confidently as dead was, in fact, very much alive. For these were the three Varro men whom Silver had sent back as messengers.

But they knew too much about El Diablo's cruel vagaries of temper to risk carrying that message. More particularly, since they could think of no convincing reason, apart from their own fear, for their not having tried to kill the Hawk where he stood. No, it had been the better part of valor to keep quiet, and pretend that they had seen and learned nothing and that their leader had been shot from afar by a dry-gulcher who had ridden off too fast for them.

Varro had scarcely taken his place before he rapped out an order, which sent the firing squad out to face the nine men.

At one edge of the crowd a big-nosed man, with a wooden leg, went tense. His hand lifted, hovering over the front of his shirt, where a suspicious looking bulge showed. The movement attracted the attention of a neighbor who glanced at this face, widened his eyes, and then gasped audibly.

Big Nose Beaujolais shot him a cold-eyed glance which effectively cut off any indiscreet speech. A soldier in the ranks just in front stared suspiciously. Big Nose disregarded him. He was about to die, and he knew it. It seemed unlikely that he would be forced to kill this soldier before he did anything else, but if that was necessary, it would be necessary, that was all.

The eyes on either side of the gargantuan nose were fixed now on Esteban Varro. The man was half-hidden by the horsemen around him, but his head could be seen, and Big Nose thought that he could hit it.

Beyond that, his plans did not go. So far as he knew, he was the last of the Trent gang. He doubted, seeing the way the prisoners were tied, whether he would be able to get them free, even in the confusion which would follow Esteban Varro's death. But in any case, Varro would be dead, and it would not be said of Big

Silver's fist whipped forward like an arcing rock.

Nose Beaujolais that he had stood aside with idle hands while his compadres were shot down.

"*On va tout de néme mourir ensemble, les gars,*" he muttered. "Anyway, we'll die together, boys."

The soldier, hearing these foreign words without understanding them, glared. Big Nose swept him with a contemptuous glance, then turned his gaze back to Varro.

In the square, the firing squad, composed of twenty-four men, came to a ragged halt, at their officer's command.

AT THE other side of the square, a steep-sided, high-wheeled cart, drawn by two mules, had pushed through the indignant crowd and had drawn up close to the line of soldiers. The cart, driven by a pale-faced peon, was piled high with hay, and on top of this hay was a dead man.

At least, he was a man who, by all the laws of Nature, should have been dead. He certainly resembled a corpse closely. He was lying down, because he was too weak to sit up, and because, also, that was a convenient way to conceal the Winchester which reposed in the hay under him.

In another incarnation this man had been called Ricardo, and when Miguel had left him for dead, he had been on his way to join Silver Trent, to run Satan out of his domain. Only, some miracle of vitality had intervened, and he had put off his trip until now. He had not the strength to get out of that cart and try to cut his comrades free, but he thought he had the strength and the steadiness of hand to kill Esteban Varro before the order to fire was given to the firing squad. In that case, his friends and himself would have some very special pleasure before they went to their deaths, and they would have some good news to take to Silver.

He fixed sunken, burning eyes on El Diablo, and began to slide the Winchester out from under him.

The ghost of Ricardo was under the impression that he alone

of Trent's men was alive and free. He had not seen the man with the big nose and the brand new peg leg, nor did he see another man who stood crouched on a roof across the way—a big, ragged-looking gaunt man, with his sombrero pulled low over eyes which, strangely for a Mexican, were gray, and who stood stooped, with one shoulder hunched higher than the other. And, though apparently a ghost, he could not see far enough through buildings to make out still other men whom he might have recognized, and the sight of which would certainly have sent new life through his emaciated bones.

Out in the square, the firing squad, at Varro's command, had raised its rifles to the loading position, and the click of the bolts sounded loud in the silence.

Ricardo had the rifle out now, its butt at his shoulder, its muzzle barely showing over the edge of the cart. Across the way, Big Nose Beaujolais slid behind his neighbor, so that the sixgun he slid out from his shirt would not be seen by the soldier.

The firing squad had their rifles at the shoulder now, and Varro had his sword raised. When it fell, they would fire.

Against the wall, one of the nine men—a lean Mexican, with a narrow, tall-browed face and burning eyes—laughed and called a blasphemous insult to the squad. "You take orders like whipped dogs," he added, "and you are as awkward as cows. Do you think you can hit the wall we stand against?"

Next to him, a man dressed impeccably in the dark clothes of a gambler turned a cool, amused glance on the speaker. "I'll give you ten to one, Pablo," he said clearly, "that they miss all of us the first try."

Doc Brimstone's hearty laugh boomed out. "By the britches of my grandfather," he said, "I'll bet they hit that popinjay with the sword before they do us."

A ripple of laughter went through the crowd, while Varro glared. Then it happened.

A crash of gunfire blared out from the top of a building nearby. The uplifted sword cut a feeble arabesque in the air and clattered to the flagstones. Four members of the firing squad staggered and went down.

THE FOLLOWING instant, Ricardo's Winchester cracked from the top of the wagon. Esteban Varro's hat leapt from his head. The driver of the cart, trembling, laid the lash on his mules and the cart leaped into motion, the high wheel smashing along the line of soldiery. On top, Ricardo's feeble curses did nothing to stop the juggernaut progress of the stampeding mules. Varro, had moved just as he shot, and Ricardo wanted another try.

Another crash of gunfire rattled from the building top. Two of the riders at Varro's side went down. Two more of the firing squad staggered under gun-shock. One of them flopped face forward. A panic-stricken voice cried, "We are betrayed! Run!"

The square was a scene of tangled confusion. Citizenry and soldiers fled in all directions, yelling, falling over one another in their haste to take cover.

At the other side of the square, a peg-legged man snapped a Colt-shot at Varro, whose black stallion was rearing and plunging madly. The shot missed. A soldier nearby turned his rifle on the gunman, took a bullet in the belly and lost interest in the proceedings.

Down toward the wall, on that same side of the square, a group of soldiers stood strangely steadfast. They neither ran nor attempted to fire. But few noticed them in that moment—neither them nor the two men who held sixguns in each hand and kept the muzzles trained so that each soldier was convinced that all four guns pointed at his own middle.

Nor did anyone notice the big, gaunt, ragged Mexican man who moved down off the roof with the swift, feral grace of a hunting cat until he was concealed behind the first of the nine prisoners against the wall. His right hand, knife-filled, moved with the speed and accuracy of a cat's paw striking.

Anyone who had seen the amazement and emotion flood up into those nine faces would have guessed that something terrific was going on, even if he had not seen the man behind them. For it wouldn't have been possible for the mere chance of escape to put such incredulous joy into those danger-hardened faces.

But no one was watching that either—not even Esteban Varro, whose bullet-creased horse was bucking him across the square and off into a side street, and whose squawled order to watch the prisoners was lost in the general uproar.

No one was watching, because this thing had happened so fast that men had not yet had time to gather their wits and think.

A new yell of terror shot up at the corner of the square. The fleeing crowd checked and scattered anew, as a group of riders with led horses shot around the corner, hoofs skittering on the pavement blocks, and drove toward the men against the wall.

There were six riders and each man led two saddled mounts. The group roared to a skidding, rearing halt. The nine prisoners, the gray-eyed "Mexican" who had cut them free, and the two other men who had held the soldiers at gunpoint, flung themselves into the saddle.

There was a milling moment while the prisoners buckled on the gunbelts which had been draped over the saddle horns. Then Silver Trent's great voice roared out.

"To me, *Los Halcones!* Hell's Hawks for Trent!"

And, guns blazing to the echo of Magpie Myers high-pitched bubbling yell of triumph, the cavalcade roared across the square toward the alley where other mounted men, the men who had joined with Silver in firing those first two volleys from the roof, were waiting to join them.

All across the square that great, legendary war-cry of Silver Trent sent the breath sucking into men's lungs, and put a thrill along their nerves. The citizens of that town of Sangre turned to stare, forgetting flight. Then the meaning of that cry got through to them and a cheer, spontaneous, full-lunged, echoing sudden joy and hope, lifted above that yelling shambles.

But down the side-street, where a black-clad man had mastered a wounded stallion, fear swept down on chilled wings. A curse, incredulous, yet bitter with sudden conviction, ripped from Esteban Varro's snarling lips. He whipped the stallion about, to send him plunging back toward the square, then checked, his dark face a study in fury and panic.

It came again, farther off now, yet clear-ringing like a blast of brazen trumpets. *"Aqui, Los Halcones!* Hell's Hawks for Trent!"

El Diablo's stricken nerves shrank into themselves. There was a sudden, deadly chill down his backbone, and an icy hand clutched his breast. For there could be no mistake in that voice. Silver Trent still lived, and the men of the Hawk rode again!

CHAPTER 8
A LESSON IN AMBUSH

ON THE outskirts of the town a high-wheeled cart, drawn by panting mules, came to an abrupt stop at the challenge of the alarmed guard there.

"Halt! Nobody's allowed out of town. Turn back!" It was a corporal at the head of a squad who spoke. His manner was excited and the rifle in his hand looked as though it were about to go off at any moment. Obviously, the shooting in the square had alarmed him.

"Señor, there is trouble," the peon driving the cart said wheedlingly. "We are but poor men, and my brother is dying. Let him see our mother before God takes him."

Suspiciously the corporal climbed onto the hub of the wheel and peered over at Ricardo. "So much at least is true," he muttered. "The man looks already like a corpse."

But on the ground again, he snarled at the driver. "My orders are to let no one pass, hombre. What has happened in the town?"

"I know nothing, Señor. Only there was shooting in the square. I drove fast because I am but a poor man and—"

"And perhaps a liar. Men, search the cart for weapons. Before I send this dog back, we will make sure that he has no teeth, eh?"

His men jumped to obey, but then froze, startled. A thunder of hoofs sounded in the dirt of the street. Some thirty men, armed and somehow fraught with danger, were roaring toward them, at full gallop.

The corporal's cheeks paled. He yelled toward two squads of his comrades, members of the cordon on either side of him, and then threw up his rifle. "Halt!" he yelled. "Halt, or I fire."

A gaunt, great-shouldered man in the lead of the cavalcade, tossed up a sixgun and sent a shot whistling over the soldiers' heads. "Give way or die!" he cried.

Shaking, the corporal dropped to one knee, lined his sights. The living skeleton on top of the cart had raised up, his eyes widening. He drew a long, shuddering breath, and sweat sprang out on his forehead. "I am dreaming," he muttered.

Then suddenly, the barrel of his Winchester jabbed out over the wagon side. "Don't shoot, amigo," he snapped at the corporal, "unless you want to die quickly."

The soldier stared, and then lowered his gun hastily. Just in time, it appeared, for the leader of the charging horsemen had leveled his Colt again, and there was death in his eyes this time.

Now, the leader lowered his gunhand, but swept the other straight up in a signal to halt. The cavalcade pulled up, excited horses rearing.

"Ricardo!" The big man's eyes were glowing, his voice husky. "And couldn't they even keep you in hell, my son?"

Ricardo's throat moved, straining, but there was no voice in him. The corporal and his men stood with their hands up now, and a shout, followed by a wild shot, came from one of the approaching squads.

A rifle cracked from the group of horsemen. The soldier

who had fired seemed to trip, then went sprawling. The others checked, and, a moment later, were racing for cover. The squad on the other side emulated them.

From the road behind, a stentorian voice boomed. *"Eh, les gars!* W'at you say, *hein?* You wait for that Beeg Nose, no?"

Fat-bellied, peg leg flapping, face radiant, Big Nose Beaujolais came racing down the street, lambasting a gaunt, unwilling mule, with what looked like a broomstick.

A cheer of welcome greeted him.

Silver turned quickly to Ricardo. "You can't ride yet, amigo? Then start those mules. We'll hold them off until you get away."

Ricardo grinned. "Geeve me ten minutes, Silver," he boasted. "These are the bes' dam mules nort' of hell. They weel ron the legs off those Varro horses."

"Good! Get going. We'll cover you."

A MOUNTED patrol of Varro men, attracted by the shots, appeared some three hundred yards away. Heartened by their presence, the foot soldiers plucked up courage enough to begin firing.

Without hesitation, Silver split his men into two groups, and charged both squads at once. It was a brief, bloodless fight. Attacked by superior numbers, the soldiers threw down their weapons and surrendered, or fled into the town.

The mounted men, however, came on. They were not new recruits but were of Varro's original fighters—gunmen who had been in his service long before he had begun to raise an army for revolution.

They came on, but they came warily, as though they suddenly sensed that these were Trent men.

There were some two score of them, so that odds were almost even. Silver frowned and bit his lip.

The cart was already on its way, racing across the plain, but he knew it would be necessary to give it a good deal more than ten minutes, unless Ricardo was to be run down and treated to some of Varro's vengeance.

For a moment, a deep reluctance tugged at him. If this did not go fast enough, his plans would be spoiled. Yet there was nothing to do.

He whipped his Winchester to his shoulder and sent a shot snarling toward the leader of Varro riders. The range was still long for accurate work with a carbine, but the bullet found the man's horse and sent him to his knees. The others checked and began firing, but their lead did no harm.

Magpie Myers' lead, on the other hand, did. The oldster dismounted, and, using his saddle as a rifle rest, sent shot after shot into the group.

One man dropped his rifle, clutching at a smashed arm. Another bullet plucked at a hat and sent it jumping off its wearer's head. A third emptied a saddle, the rider falling as though he had been hit by a club. The horse, a likely looking animal, stampeded off onto the plain.

Beside his mule, Big Nose Beaujolais grinned and cut a caper on his wooden-leg.

"*Voila mon cheval!*" he boomed. "By Gar, I weel ron dis leetle horse down, an' den I weel geeve back dis mule to de damn robber I hav' stole heem from. May hees children be born wit' long ears, de *voleur*. Hees mules is no damn good."

A column of infantry debouched suddenly from the square, and came at the double down the street. They gave to one side almost at once to allow the passage of some forty or fifty horsemen.

Silver shot a quick, estimating glance out over the plain to where Ricardo's cart was setting up a plume of dust. His big hands clenched and a sudden, agonized sweat sprang out on his forehead.

Gracia was still in this town, in Padre Pete's house. Silver had forbidden her to take part in the rescue of the prisoners, believing that the chances of the effort succeeding were too slim. He had hoped for the panic which had come on the heels of the first volley, and it had been one of his men, planted in the crowd, who had set up the terror-stricken cry of treachery. But such complete success had seemed too much to hope for. And if there had been any sort of quick-witted and organized resistance, that square might have been turned into a holocaust of death.

Yet, once the attempt was started, he had to ride out with his men, at least until they were safe. He had intended to leave them within a few minutes of their escape from the town, and return for Gracia, counting on his own ingenuity to get her out before Varro had time for a search which would bring that presence to light. Now, every minute increased her danger.

Nonetheless, he had to help Ricardo, and now that his men were pressed by a greatly outnumbering force of Varro riders, it was clearly his duty to stick with them.

For a long moment, he sat rigid, fighting the weakness which bade him listen to his fears for the girl he loved and forget the fate of the men who served him.

It was a memory which swung the balance—the memory of Gracia beside him at the barricade, of the certainty which had come over him then that if she was to share his life she would have to share its dangers also. He could not swerve from the things that made him Silver Trent, nor would she want him to.

Imperceptibly, his muscles relaxed and the strain went out of the corners of his mouth. He turned to his waiting men.

"Spread out," he said crisply, "and ride after the cart. We'll turn and fight when we've gotten out of range of those buzzards on foot."

AT SIGHT of their retreat, the two groups of Varro riders set up a shout and put spurs to their horses.

Silver smiled grimly to himself. In the open, fight and run, he had no fear that his men could not take care of themselves, His regular riders were experts at that game, could out-think, outride and out-shoot any killer Varro had been able to hire, and this new bunch looked like the right material. They had fought magnificently at the barricade, and they had behaved like old-timers during the affair at the square. His thanks went out to Padre Pete for his shrewdness and judgment of men. Through him, Silver had the makings of a gang just about as large and as formidable as he had had before.

It took only a little while to show that his confidence was justified. At the first stand they made, El Diablo's riders were forced to give back. After some delay, they split and attempting a flanking movement, hoping evidently to throw a ring around Silver and his men and keep them in a trap until the foot soldiers could come. But they only lost time by that, for Silver could move back in a straight line a good deal faster than they could circle.

Within an hour, the retreat had reached the rising ground toward the hills. The infantry had been left so far behind that it was out of sight, and the cart containing Ricardo had long since disappeared.

Half an hour later found them in broken country, with both their advantage and their danger increased. If El Diablo's riders managed to split and, under cover of some ravine, get in behind them, they would be in a bad fix. On the other hand, their own chances for concealment and cover were vastly increased.

AHEAD, THE trail ran through a shallow, rising valley which was blocked on the far end by a brush covered ridge. Beyond the ridge, the ground dipped, then rose steadily, so that it was possible to see the winding of the trail at intervals for a mile or more.

Once over the ridge, Silver called a halt and held a grim, half-unspoken parley with Magpie. A moment later, a party of six men moved forward along the trail. Seen on any one of the visible sections of it, they would be taken for a rear guard, and the other men would appear to be ahead of them.

Actually, the remaining men dismounted and took cover in the brush on the slope of the ridge, the horses being held back out of sight.

They had only a few minutes to wait. El Diablo's riders,

conscious of their greatly superior force, had been pressing them closely, sparring for an advantage in this game of hit and run. Now, they came on with relaxed caution.

At the foot of the slope, the leader shouted and pointed. Evidently, they had seen the half dozen men who had been sent on ahead, for at a signal, the whole force swept forward at a gallop.

They were met by a withering blast from the bushes. It piled them up in a kicking, squealing shambles of hit horses and hurt and yelling men. Instead of instantly leaving their saddles and taking cover, panic swept them and they raced off down the trail.

By the time they recovered and reorganized for an advance, Silver and his men were back over the top of the ridge and in the saddle. From then on, they rode fast, but without much concern. The pursuit would be too slow and cautious now to trouble them. With that lesson under their belts, Varro's men would scout every possible place for an ambush along the trail before going ahead.

Some ten miles farther on, Silver pulled up. "I've got a job to do," he said briefly to Magpie. "Ride on to the hideout. I hear that Varro has about twenty men on guard there to keep anybody from getting out, but he hasn't found the back way in. Don't risk a fight. Go in by the rear trail and wait. I expect to be back within twenty-four hours."

Magpie's gaze clouded and he opened his mouth to speak. But the habit of not questioning Silver's decisions was ingrained in him. He ended by nodding and leading the crowd on.

Silver rode off the trail, following a rocky gully until he

reached a high point some half mile away. There he waited until the Varro riders came by, the shadow of a smile tugging at his grim lips as he noted the caution with which they advanced. In the course of ten miles, his own crowd had pulled ahead by nearly an hour.

He waited until the slow cavalcade had gotten well out of sight and then took the back trail.

CHAPTER 9
THE ENEMY CAMP

S UNSET FOUND Silver dismounting in front of a hut that was hidden in a fold of the hills on the other side of Sangre. And an hour later, when dusk had fallen over the town, he was at the outskirts of Sangre. Only, now, the ragged, bare-footed peon had given way to quite another individual—a mustachioed Mexican caballero, all swagger and magnificence.

A sentry at the end of the street challenged, and Silver pulled up. He lifted a hand in a greeting that was full of fine bravado.

"Hola, compadre," he called. "Is it here that I will find Don Esteban Varro?"

The sentry, who walked with something of a stagger, attempted to stiffen.

"And what do you want with *El General Varro?*" he growled.

"Eh! Eh! *El General!* Then it is true, what I hear of this revolution. Men say that a real fighting man will find a full meal of action in the service of *El General Varro*. And I, amigo"—Silver slapped his chest in a grandiose gesture—"am a son of war itself. Tell me where the headquarters are. You see before you a comrade at arms!"

The sentry peered at him through the darkness. An expression bordering on respect came over his drink-flushed features. For what he saw before him lent force to the newcomer's words. This man looked like what he said he was—a warrior, from the high, pointed crown of his emblazoned hat to the heels of his silver-spurred boots. Over those boots flared wide-bottomed trousers, richly embroidered in gold, narrowed at the knee and tight over muscular thighs. Over a silk shirt and a bolero equally impressive crossed cartridge belts banded a proudly swelling chest. And beneath the wide curled brim of the sombrero was a fierce face, the principal features of which were a long, belligerently upcurled black mustache and flashing eyes which appeared as black. Some bandido from the south, no doubt, come to offer his services and share in the loot of the revolution.

Yes, from the south surely, and a *caballero,* for the sonorous, faultless Spanish had the lisping Castilian sibilant which were affected by the gentlemen of Mexico City.

The sentry brought his rifle up in what he hoped was a smart salute. "Pass, comrade," he said. "You will find headquarters in the *Alcaldía* in the *Plaza Centrale.*"

Silver thanked him in a grandiloquent phrase and went on. But needless to say he did not go to the *Alcaldía.* He knew his disguise was a thin one at best. It would be penetrated without difficulty by anyone who was at all familiar with his appearance.

The streets, as he rode along, presented a lively appearance. It was obvious that Varro's men were celebrating their "victory," and that a large proportion of the citizenry were joining in with them. Cafés and cantinas blazed with light and from them a warring confusion of music and boisterous voices issued— guitars competing discordantly with the tin-pan notes of mechanical pianos, and a general hubbub of boasting, rejoicing or quarrelsome speech.

Silver rode boldly along the main street leading to the square. He dismounted beyond it, in front of a cantina which was not far from the alley that led to Padre Pete's house. A glance inside the cantina showed him no one he knew, though the place was crowded, so he swaggered in and called loudly for *tequila.*

"What say, comrade?" he boomed at the greasy individual who served him, "We make a glorious beginning, do we not?"

"Por Dios, yes, Señor," the man replied subserviently.

One of Varro's soldiers turned a drunken gaze his way. "Hola! You are one of us, comrade?"

"I? Ask Esteban Varro if *Miguel de la Costa* was not one of his men—men of old! I fought with him, friend, before this new army was thought of."

The soldier looked a little abashed, but Silver clapped him on the shoulder and insisted that they drink together. The crowd, which had fallen silent at his entrance, began its talk again, and while pretending to chat with the soldier Silver kept both ears open.

FROM SNATCHES here and there, Silver gathered that his own sensational reappearance that morning and the rescue of his men still continued to be the news of the hour. But the general opinion seemed to be that he could do little harm to

Varro, if, indeed, he had not already been caught by the pursuing riders. Of Padre Pete and Gracia he heard nothing, and, after a few moments, he went out.

He walked up the street toward the alley, with his heart hammering now in his chest and his nerves drawn taut as stretched wires. Had Gracia and Padre Pete been caught? Would he be able to find them? Was the Padre's house watched?

At the mouth of the alley, he began to stagger and burst into drunken song.

Ahead of him, the high wall in the rear of the house's garden lifted blank and shimmering pallidly in the starlight. He dared not attempt to climb over it, not knowing what he would find on the other side. So he staggered on to the front, still singing his maudlin, raucous song.

His eyes, searching under his sombrero, could find no sign that the house was being watched, nor any sign of life inside. At the door, he staggered still more, and sat down heavily, as though he could no longer stand. Sprawling there, he waited a few minutes, watching. Then he began to sing softly a song that he and Gracia had often sung together, "Cielito Lindo."

A window nearby opened cautiously, and a soft voice breathed hesitantly, "Who are you?"

Silver stood up and said quietly, "Hello, my dear. Will you open the door for me?"

He heard her breath go out as she became sure of him, and a second later the door opened.

He closed the door behind him and swept her into his arms.

Working fast, Silver ripped off the soldier's clothes and got
into the uniform. He tied and gagged him.

Standing there in the dark, the flood of relief in him loosened
the grip of his nerves, set his great body to trembling suddenly.

"My dear, my dear!" Gracia's voice was broken. "You've done
too much after being so sick. You must lie down and rest."

He got himself together. "No," he said quietly. "No. I'm all
right. Where's Padre Pete?"

From the darkness behind Gracia, the priest's voice sounded,
a little shaken. "I am here, my son."

They told him that they had thought the house was being

watched, but that it might not be so. Varro had made a thorough search for them, or rather for the Padre, for he did not seem to know that Gracia was there, but might have concluded that he had escaped along with the others. He and Gracia had hidden in the old church crypt, over which the house had been built, and so had escaped during the search of the house itself. They had heard no news of Varro's plans.

"I've got to circulate around and see what I can find out," Silver said, his voice sounding curiously uncertain. "Then I'll come back and we'll all three get out of town."

"Oh, no—no!" Gracia cried. "Please, Silver. You—you've crowded your luck today. Something bad will come of it. I—I feel it."

Silver's nails bit into his palms. The words aroused a premonition that was already in his own mind. He had pushed his luck hard that day, he knew. He had left Gracia here in danger that made him sick to think of. The temptation to get her out now, without risking anything more, was almost irresistible. For a long second, that shaking came back into his limbs again, and the jerk of his nerves crying, "Get out—get out quick, before it's too late!" was an unendurable thing.

He took a long breath, and then said, his voice steel-level and quiet, "I've got to go. I won't have such a chance again, maybe. But I'll be back. Wait here for me."

A moment later, he was in the street again, the girl's soft, broken sob and Padre Pete's tranquil blessing a double ringing in his ears.

LIKE A shadow, he moved away from the house, and then

84

took on a drunken swagger, not so maudlinly pronounced now, but enough to make him look like a celebrant. He headed for the Plaza Centrale and went boldly into the noisiest and most crowded of the bars.

The square itself swarmed with soldiers and citizens. Even the girls had come out of hiding. The people, not only out of diplomacy, but also out of the native weakness for any kind of a fiesta were joining in the celebration.

Inside the cantina, a three-piece orchestra played, men and women danced on a side floor, several roulette and faro games were in progress and the bar itself was so crowded that a man had to elbow his way in to get a drink. The air was filled with a great babble of talk, and was thick with the smoke of innumerable cigarettes.

Grinning, still playing the good-humored drunk, Silver pushed his way in and commanded *tequila*, not only for himself but for the half a dozen men nearest him. A soldier, with what appeared to be sergeant's stripes on his arm looked at him and winked, as Silver began to talk about their glorious victory and the good things in store for anyone who followed Esteban Varro. His talk, and the fact that he had bought liquor for others, was, apparently, the only passport he needed as one of Varro's men.

The reason for that readily became apparent. Every Varro man in the place was buying drinks for everybody. Plainly, they had been supplied with money and with orders to entertain in the town. El Diablo, to cover his humiliation of the morning, was bent on buying popularity, as well, no doubt, as gaining actual recruits.

One befuddled and child-like citizen was asking if he would get a uniform and a rifle by enlisting.

The sergeant clapped him boisterously on the shoulder. "Never fear for that, amigo," he declared. "A new shipment of uniforms just came in today. They are held at our headquarters up in the mountains, where there were still a few hundred men who were not equipped. There'll be plenty of uniforms for all."

"There are other men, then, up in the mountains?"

"Others?" The sergeant loosed a braying laugh. "Several thousand, *amigo*. Did you think that *El General* would use his whole army for a small affair like this? You can see for yourself that the people are for us. If it had not been for those rascally thieves who followed this Silver Trent, there would have been no blood shed at all."

"Thousands? Do you mean it?" The prospective recruit looked impressed. "But the rifles—there cannot be guns for all."

The sergeant winked at him. "Never fear for that, compadre." He lowered his voice to give what he said a confidential air. "A big new shipment of arms is on its way right this minute," he announced. "I will not tell you where it is or when it will arrive. That would not be discreet, eh, friend? But it will be here soon." He raised his voice and made a wide gesture. "Arms for all—for everybody," he proclaimed. "Ah, you can't beat our *General*. He is irresistible, I tell you."

"Maybe *El Halcon* will have something to say about that," a voice cut in from the crowd.

The sergeant glared, but before he could reply, a big, brutal-mouthed man in the uniform of an officer reached out and got the offending speaker by the front of his shirt.

"So! You are a friend of that dog of a cattle thief!" he snarled. "We have ways of dealing with your kind."

The man had been drunk enough to speak incautiously, but he was not so drunk as to be unable to appreciate the mistake he had made. His cheeks paled and stark fear was suddenly in his eyes.

"I—I meant no harm, *Señor Capitan*," he stammered. "I—it is only what I have heard said. For my part I—"

The officer gave him a savage shake and then released him. "See that you keep a civil tongue in your head, then," he growled.

"These so-called Hawks are already dead men." The officer was speaking now to the crowd. "Our brave fellows have them trapped and surrounded in the hills. Silver Trent, himself, is gravely wounded. They will be taken soon, and then you will have the pleasure of seeing them and their leader hanged in the *Plaza Centrale*."

"It is true. I have heard it myself, only half an hour ago," a credulous citizen put in.

CHAPTER 10
CORNERED!

UNDER HIS flowing mustache, Silver's dark-stained lips moved in an involuntary smile. From this welter of report, rumor and lies it was difficult to sort out any truth. But one thing had set his pulses suddenly hammering.

The sergeant had said something about an arms shipment. The thing might be wholly mythical, but on the other hand, if it were true, it would solve the problem which was giving Silver his greatest concern. If Esteban Varro was to be defeated, it would need an army to do it, and that army would have to be armed.

The problem of raising men to fight against El Diablo did not worry Silver. The man's reputation for greed and ruthless cruelty was so well known that the moment a real chance showed to topple his revolution there would be recruits in plenty. But without arms, there was no chance. And Silver up to now had no way to get arms.

He cursed silently at the memory of the bullion shipment which he had failed to re-take from Varro. It had been that money, no doubt, which had enabled El Diablo to furnish out an army. Yet, if there was a new shipment of arms coming in, and it was possible to intercept them....

Someway, Silver's racing mind affirmed, he would have to learn the truth, get details. But how? Where? Then it came to him that he would have to go to the *Alcaldía* after all! There, if anywhere, he could find the information he sought. Somewhere among the headquarters papers there would be a notification, orders. If he could find them....

He stood there, with his fingers digging into the wood of the bar, his thoughts so intense that he had small ear for the talk around him. At headquarters there would be plenty of men who knew his appearance well. It would not be long before somebody penetrated his disguise. Moreover, the offices would be guarded. The town officials had fled and Varro had appointed new ones of his own. No doubt, headquarters, even at this hour, would be a hive of activity. His chance of getting what he wanted would be one in a thousand. Yet, he must try. Thank God, so far he had not been recognized. Part of his strength would lie in the fact that people expected him to be anywhere but here in Sangre.

"...that *El General* will take the girl who was Silver Trent's mistress?"

The words cut through Silver and sent a sudden vein thrusting out on his forehead. That could only mean Gracia.

The officer, in whose cold eyes one incautious citizen had read instant death, opened his brutal mouth in a sneering laugh. "Silver Trent's mistress? Do you think that *El General* would content himself with such a one? She who was at the beck and call of the whole crew of them? *El General* will throw her to his soldiers and then string her up along with the false priest who procured her."

Silver's body moved faster than his thought. "You dirty-mouthed, lying dog!" his bitter lips ripped out savagely, and his fist whipped forward like an arcing rock.

At his words, the officer had whirled to face him, so that the blow caught him full. His head snapped back against his spine. His big body hurtled into the crowd, smashing through, and hit the floor full-length with a thud.

For an instant, there was stunned immobility. The whipping, unbelievable power behind that punch, the spurting, crushing impact of it, held men in a kind of startled awe. Then citizens and some of the soldiery began to stampede away from the vicinity, tumbling over one another in their haste to get out of reach of that gaunt, blazing-eyed man who stood there, armed and deadly angry.

On the floor, the officer lay as though he were dead.

"Por Dios, it is no wonder if his neck is broken," someone gasped.

But Silver knew, with a swift, unreasoning regret, that the man still lived. The continuing pulse of blood proved that. Silver's great fist had smashed his nose into the likeness of a crushed tomato, had split his upper lip in half and knocked out his upper front teeth. He would never look the same again, but he would not die.

The sergeant had backed hastily away, until he stood side by side with a thin-faced man who was staring at Silver with the deadly, unwinking eyes of a snake—as though he saw in him some familiarity that puzzled him. They were to one side of Silver, apparently out of range of his vision.

Suddenly, the thin-faced man drew in his breath sharply, hesitated a shaken fraction of a second, then stabbed swiftly, furtively, for his gun. His narrow, unwinking eyes were suddenly filled with murder.

SILVER'S BODY did not move. Only, his left hand flicked with blinding speed. He shot once, across his stomach. The snake-eyed man cried out in pain and fear. His left hand clutched at a smashed shoulder, while his right released the sixgun he had half-drawn. The gun toppled out of its holster onto the floor.

Both Silver's Colts were in his hands now, and he was backing toward the door, the gray-tawny blaze of his eyes holding the crowd immobile even more than the guns did.

"If no one moves, no one will die, *amigos,*" his stirred voice flung at them, vibrant and warning.

A civilian in the crowd was staring at him goggle-eyed, his throat working. It was that man who had said, "Maybe *El Halcon* will have something to say about that."

Now speech, shaken and involuntary, burst from between his parted lips. "By the blood of Christ," he gasped, "that is Silver Trent!" And then went deadly pale, because his tongue had betrayed him.

A gust of indrawn breath whipped about the room.

"He's right," someone breathed. "In the Blessed Virgin's name, where were my eyes?"

Silver's expression did not change, but a bitter curse rolled up into his mind, as he backed out of the door and whirled to run. He had done it now. Within minutes, Varro's whole force would be a hornet's nest about his ears.

Inside the saloon, the breathless tension held a long second after he had disappeared, then a voice ripped up, awed, half-hysterical, "That is no man—that is more than a man!"

"*Carramba!*" another burst out, "but you are right! How can he be holed up in the hills and here at one and the same minute. If my eyes had not seen…."

A cyclone of excited agreement whipped about the room. "God! Did you see that speed?"… "Hombre, it was the eyes— the eyes! Like some god's."… "True! I could not face them, yet they held me."… "And here, through the guards. *Amigos,* I tell you not even stone walls and bars could hold back such a one. If I were Esteban Varro I would not sleep well this night!"

Then a soldier, the sergeant, burst out the door, racing across the square with the news. As though it were a signal, the whole cantina emptied, babbling, the crowd beside itself with excitement.

Silver, once outside the door, had darted down the side street. Circling, he reached the back of the *Alcaldía*, which was opposite the cantina, before the racing soldier got there.

The building ran through, from the square to the street behind. In the rear, a high wall enclosed what appeared to be a patio behind the main building. A small door was the only entrance, and before this door a sentry paced up and down, a bayoneted rifle on his shoulder.

It was a street of small stores, which had been closed and shuttered for the night. No doubt their proprietors were out taking advantage of the free drinks which flowed everywhere.

Silver had no time to lose, so he did a simple thing. He walked up to the sentry, staggering and grinning in drunken good humor, and then smashed him in the jaw with his fist.

The man went limp, but Silver caught him before he fell and carried him under one arm across the street to the mouth of a dark alley. There, working fast, he ripped off the soldier's clothes, and got into the uniform. The coat instantly split-across the back and the trousers ended half-way down from his knees, but there was no help for that.

Dressed, he tied the man with his belt and gagged him with his bandanna. It would not keep him long, but Silver could not bring himself to slap the man behind the ear with a sixgun, as he knew he should have done.

He found the door in the *Alcaldía* wall locked, and had to pry it open with the sentry's bayonet. It yielded with a screech of metal. Silver stepped through, fast. Once in, his breath went out in a swift sigh of relief, for the patio was empty. No one had heard the lock break.

HE CROSSED swiftly and silently to the rear of the building. A lighted window showed him an empty office, a desk piled high with papers.

He stepped through the window and cat-footed to the desk. His fingers shook a little as they leafed through the piles of papers, but they moved with swift accuracy nonetheless. And as they moved, his eyes flicked and his brain snapped, taking in the contents of the papers.

He had come to the end of the first pile and was half through the second, with his heart getting lower and lower, when voices sounded in the hall. The click of booted heels sounded just outside the room in which he stood.

He had not time to get back through the window, and a swift glance showed him that the room was devoid of cover, except for the desk before which he stood It stood across the angle of a corner, and there was room there for a man to squeeze in. Instantly, Silver vaulted it, sank out of sight just as two men came in the door.

Their voices sounded excited and angry, and the first words told Silver that they had all heard of his presence in town.

"I tell you, *Commandante,*" one of them said next, *"El General* had better get the escort going for that arms shipment and he had better make it big. With that devil of a Trent loose, there's no telling what will happen. The man is more than human."

"You're right," the other replied grimly, "and the General knows it. He's already given orders that the escort is to march tonight at midnight. The shipment was due to reach Coahuila Border tomorrow at dusk, near the ford of the Rio Amarillo, but Varro is taking no chances. We are to cross the river and meet the packtrain as far down the Aguas Negros valley as possible. I'm taking two hundred riders. With the gun-runners themselves that ought to be enough, even for Silver Trent."

Behind the desk, Silver held his breath, his pulses hammering with exultation. Luck? Who said his luck had run out? And then instantly, his blood froze.

Racing footsteps echoed in the hall and a voice cried out, *Commandante, Commandante!* They've found somebody in the priest's house."

"What? You are sure?" The *Commandante's* voice snapped with excitement.

"Sure! A moment ago, two persons went in the front door."

"Carramba, hombre! What are you waiting for? Take half a hundred men and surround the house, as quietly as you can. Then break in fast, and capture them. Maybe Trent himself is in there."

Silver could have groaned aloud. He guessed what had happened. Gracia, uneasy, and maybe hearing excitement in the square, had insisted on going out to find out what had happened to him. Now there would be no end to the search until they were found....

Silver came to his feet in one swift, cat-like movement.

"Don't move or make any noise," he said softly.

The two officers were goggling at him open-mouthed.

"What—what is the meaning of this, soldier?" the *Comman-dante* got out.

Silver put a hand on the desk and vaulted over.

The other man's face had gone suddenly pale. His mouth worked, but no speed came out of it.

Silver went out the window in one swift bound, and heard the man's strangled whisper in the room behind him. "It's Trent— Trent!"

CHAPTER 11
WHEN GHOST GUNS RIDE

S ILVER RACED for the gate. As he tore around the building, he could hear a voice crackling orders in front and the confused movements of soldiers preparing to fall in. He raced across the open, hurtled through the crowd in the main street and darted into the alley behind the padre's house.

By the rear wall, two figures stirred. One of them sung out a quick challenge.

He ran toward them calling out that they were to get around in front, on the double.

A tense voice answered, "Who says so, hombre? Who are you?"

Starlight gleamed on a leveled rifle barrel.

"You fool," Silver snapped, "I come with orders."

The guard waited half a second too long. When he saw that Silver did not stop before him but was coming in fast, his finger tightened spasmodically on the trigger.

Silver's left arm swung out and upward. The rifle barrel snapped up as charge exploded. Muzzle-flame seared Silver's cheek and the report seemed blast his ear drums out.

The barrel of the sixgun in his right hand smashed square into the guard's face. Both went earthward together, Silver's momentum carrying him.

The other guard's rifle blasted over Silver's head as he went down. On the ground, Silver twisted, coming to his feet, but the guard had not taken time to lever another shell into his gun. Instead, he clubbed it, and Silver looked up to see the butt whistling down for his head. The sixgun in his hand blasted once.

The gun butt, deflected a little as the wielder's body jerked to that belly shot, hit Silver on the shoulder. Instantly, he shot to his feet. The man he had hit in the face was dazed but not out. Tight-lipped, Silver clipped him behind the ear with the barrel of the sixgun, whirled, backed against the far side of the alley and then sent his great body forward in one power-driven, cat-like leap. His iron fingertips caught the edge of the high wall and held like grappling hooks.

An instant later he was dropping into the patio. At the back door of the house a figure stirred in the shadows, disappearing.

"Padre Pete!" Silver's whisper cut the darkness.

The priest reappeared instantly. His tranquil voice had a hint of a smile in it as he said, "You don't look the same, my son."

"Get Gracia. The ladder, quick! Where is it?" Silver panted.

Gracia was behind the priest and it was her figure, swift-moving as mercury, that caught and put the ladder against the wall.

Silver had heard shouts and running footsteps from the front of the house. Now, other shouts were coming from the square. In a moment, they would be cut off.

"Follow me, quickly," he breathed, and swarmed up the ladder.

As he hit the top of the wall, he heard a man give a startled exclamation just below, and heard another come running from the corner.

The scrape of Silver's boot as he hit the top of the wall brought a face below snapping upward, startled. Then Silver's big body hurtled downward.

The guard below gave a startled squawk and tried to raise his rifle, but he was too late. Silver hit him like a catapult, driving him to ground and knocking the breath out of his body.

The other man stopped short and flung up his rifle, snapping a lightning shot at Silver as he came up from the ground, whirling. The bullet plucked at his shirt sleeve.

Silver's sixgun bucked twice against his palm. The dark figure in the alley wavered like a wind-blown candle shadow and then crumpled. Gracia was hanging by her fingers from the wall. Now she dropped. An instant later, Padre Pete followed her.

Silver caught the girl by the arm and raced for the street. He had left his horse outside the cantina, and there were others at the hitchrack. The three hit the saddle in one swift rush.

The guard gave a startled squawk as Silver hurtled down upon him.

In the crowd, someone cried out in sharp protest. Evidently, this was the owner of one of the horses. At the corner of the square, a column of soldiers debouched into the street, running.

The Varro rider who had cried out, was going for his gun.

"Ride!" Silver snapped to the girl and the Padre.

Their horses whirled, hoofs thundering. The Varro rider's gun was out.

Silver sent one shot smashing into his shoulder, and then swung his horse on his hind hoofs and jumped him into a dead run.

The street had cleared like magic. Behind Silver, the officer in charge of the soldiers bellowed an order.

"Around the first corner." Silver yelled to the pair in front, and then bent low in the saddle.

A blasting volley sounded behind. Lead howled and snarled around him. He held his breath, but neither Gracia nor the Padre showed signs of having been hit. An instant later, they flashed around the corner, and before the next volley came, Silver also was out of sight.

At the edge of town, Silver's sixgun leapt into his hand and his mouth went grim. But no guard challenged. It was only after they had gotten by, that a drunken figure raised itself from the shadows and called some maudlin curse after them....

THE DAYS that followed were to go down in the history of the Sierras Pequeñas country as more packed with stark drama than any others in the memory of men.

By noon the next day, reports of Silver's exploits, garbled and exaggerated in the telling, had spread from one end of the country to the other, with that miraculous speed of the grape-vine telegraph which no one has ever been able satisfactorily to explain.

Sangre itself seethed and bubbled with excitement and specu-lation. Wild rumors swept across the town like successive waves of prairie fire. From the countryside roundabout, a constant influx of the curious swelled the babbling crowds in the streets and bars.

Varro was known to have left town at midnight at the head of two hundred riders, his dark face a mask of frustrated fury, his eyes so deadly venomous that men quailed from their impact.

Throughout the town ran whispered tales of the man's insane raging the night before. Already beside himself because of the loss of the nine prisoners and the knowledge that Silver Trent still lived, Silver's reappearance and successful escape with the priest and the girl had thrown him into a state bordering on apoplexy.

No one knew the reason for the midnight march, but it was assumed that he had taken the trail of his enemy. His soldiers announced belligerently that the Hawk's nest and everyone in it would be destroyed before night fell, but there was a notable lack of conviction in their voices. Wherever ordinary men gathered together the opinion was open that if any one was destroyed it would be Varro and not Silver Trent.

The awe which had greeted his reappearance in the cantina that night had not lessened as rumors of his other exploits had gained currency. Indeed, from that moment in the saloon, when someone had declared that he was more than a man, had been born the legend, which was to persist and strengthen, among the ignorant and superstitious, that Silver Trent was in reality a supernatural being, a kind of lesser god, impervious to the attempts and the bullets of merely human men.

By noon of that day also, news of the revolt in the Sierras Pequeñas had sifted through to the capitol. Grave-faced men in Mexico City sat about a table, reviling the impossibility of getting reinforcements to the district in time to do any good, and murmuring the name of Silver Trent in tones that varied between doubt and hope.

There might have been more hope than doubt if they could have seen the man they talked of.

For at noon that day, Silver Trent himself sat his horse on a promontory high above the valley of the Aguas Negros, and smiled grimly as he watched a pack train wind its way among the boulders on the rocky floor below.

At his side, Magpie Myers swore explosively. "Must be more'n a hundred mules," he exclaimed. "Plenty for a thousand rifles an' ammunition!"

Silver nodded. His eyes were deep-socketed, red-rimmed, set in a gray-gaunt face, but they glowed now as though there were no fatigue in the man. Yet he had not slept for more than forty-eight hours, and he had been active enough to exhaust half a dozen men.

That night, he and Gracia and the Padre had all but killed three horses on a breakneck ride to the hideout. And within five minutes of their arrival, Silver, at the head of all his men, had led the way out on another killing ride to beat Varro to the rendezvous with the gun-train.

A MOMENT longer, Silver watched the train, crawling forward like a small, segmented worm. Then he cast a glance up the valley.

Nothing moved there in the yonder distance save the heat-waves shimmering above baked and barren rocks. There was no sign of Esteban Varro's men. Silver wondered if the *Commandante* had remembered how much he had said within the hearing of a man crouched behind his desk, and whether or not he had dared to tell Varro of it.

Presently, Silver turned to look at his men. They were there behind him in a compact group—familiar faces, their eyes speaking to his, their lean, wolf-like bodies easy in the saddle— Pablo, whose prayers in peace and whose blasphemies in action must have pretty nearly canceled one another, but whose naming loyalty would surely win him a place, one day, on the right hand of his beloved saints; Ricardo, in the saddle where he should not be, upheld by the sheer flame of his joy in this reunion of the gang; Doc Brimstone, fighting a new recurrence of his perennial hangover; Beau Buchanan, looking, after nearly a dozen hours hard riding, as though he had newly stepped out of a band-box; Big Nose Beaujolais, carrying his peg leg like a jaunty decoration; Miguel, Carlos, Jim Clane, Lars Johanssen, half a dozen others, stamped with the hallmark of the Hawk.

And with these, fifteen new faces, hardbitten, proven already in one grueling, man-testing fight. Good men. Even now, a new thing showed in them—a pride, a sense of caste and loyalty, a borning swagger—the first faint imprint of the Hawk's mold.

Yet seeing, them, Silver's eyes clouded a little, for they made him remember the faces that were not there. The men who, on just such a raid as this, had ridden at his side to their last, long rendezvous with Death.

It was Ricardo who spoke then, Ricardo, who had come back from the dead and who knew the mind of Silver Trent as Miguel had once known it.

"They ride with us, Silver," he said. "Not one, but is true to his oath. Ghost guns at our side, and their hearts high because we ride again."

"Aye!" Miguel's voice seconded him, while his teeth flashed in a reckless grin. "They but wait to hear that great laugh of yours, and they'll spit in the face of Death and kick Hell's devils out of their path as they ride to join us."

Then, for the first time, the constricting band lifted wholly from around Silver Trent's heart and the old reckless lightness rode with him. His gaunt features brightened and because of the full relief in him, he tipped back his head and laughed, as he had not expected to laugh again, full-throated, in the clear, fearless gaiety of a man who has found himself.

His laughter echoed back to him, there among the rocks, so that it was as though there were ghostly voices chuckling in answer. Then he swung his horse to the downward trail.

"We ride," he said, and laughed again.

That was at noon.

CHAPTER 12
THE BATTLE IN
THE BADLANDS

I T WAS two hours later when Esteban Varro, at the head of a small army, reached a spot in the Aguas Negros where half a hundred hang-dog mule-drivers, a-foot and stripped of their arms, plodded sullenly along the rocky valley floor.

Telling of that, afterwards, men remembered that this time Varro neither raged nor cursed. He sat silent, with his mouth gone dead white, and his eyes blank and withdrawn, as though they looked into some private, future hell which only he could see. After a little, a shiver ran through his body. Wordless, he turned and led his men on the back trail.

Behind him, his riders exchanged queer glances. They themselves knew that the chances of trailing Silver Trent and finding him in that country, when he had a two hours' start, were one in a hundred. The ability of the Hawk's crew to cover a trail and lose themselves as though they had dropped from the face of the earth was famous, and uncanny. Yet not to take that one chance in a hundred, when so much was at stake....

They rode with tightened lips and a doubt crawling like a maggot through their minds.

What they did not know was that Esteban Varro had considered the possibility of finding Silver and the guns and had known that even the finding would be a fatal mistake. Two hundred men might be enough to protect the guns, if Varro himself had them, but they were not enough to fight through the ambushes that Silver Trent would set for them. And Varro's prestige could not stand any more unsuccessful brushes with his enemy.

Even as it was, the story of the capture of the guns leaked out and spread like wild-fire, not only through the countryside, but through El Diablo's own forces. A steady flow of desertions began, as men who served through fear and greed began to believe that they had chosen the wrong side of the affair.

Half a dozen prompt and savage executions did much to stop that flow, but the unease and the uncertainty persisted, below the surface.

Yet Esteban Varro was a long way from licked. That moment of apparent weakness when he discovered the loss of his arms shipment was succeeded by a fury of savage energy. Faced with his first desertions, he called his troops together and gave them a talk.

"We've lost a few hundred rifles," he shouted, "—a drop in the bucket. We'll have more, and plenty of them, and fast! The cow-thief who stole that one small shipment, won't be able to do anything with them. Where are the men to use them? Every real fighting man in this countryside is in sight of my eyes right this minute! What are left? House dogs! Not fit to whip with your belts! Suppose that Silver Trent manages to put some false courage into a few of them—we'll wipe them from the face of the earth in the first real fight. The revolution is won! Already we have taken one important town. Wait with courage, my soldiers, and be ready to go forward with courage when the time comes. The government in Mexico City is far away. They can do nothing. The Federal troops have already shown that they do not dare and do not wish to resist us. You will see soon that they are our allies. Nothing can resist you. Victory is yours."

From the close-packed throng of more than two thousand men, a wild cheer lifted. The magnetism of the man, his strength, and the very evil shrewdness and certainty in him, had converted them. It fired them with a new enthusiasm. If he could make good on his promises, they were not likely to doubt him again.

As a follow-up, he let it be known that the Federal troops in the district had already been bought off. Convinced that resistance was useless, they had made a virtue of necessity and given their tacit consent to Varro's conquest. Some of them were going actively to join his forces. And those who did not had agreed to remain idle, to lend their passive encouragement. In this way, the final triumph was certain.

And, indeed, it seemed so. Even the awe which surrounded the name of Silver Trent paled before this open-and-shut setup. **IN FACT,** even Silver was far from confident of the ultimate issue. Once the exultation which followed the capture of the arms had worn off, he began to ask himself what, after all, he would be able to do with them. Raising an army, without money, and in the face of such powerful opposition, was not such an easy thing to do.

Back in the Hawk's Nest, with the rifles, the ammunition and the two Gatling guns, which had formed an unexpected and heartening part of the loot, he called his tired men together.

"So far, my sons," he said, "we have been lucky. We have guns, but without men to use them, we are no better off than we were before. What can we do? Can anyone say how we are to raise the army we need?"

Pablo, his lean face afire, yet almost contemptuous, threw up his head. "Men?" he cried. "Is it men you want, *Jefe? Sangre de Cristo!* Give me a few hours and I will send them pouring in here until you beg me to stop them!"

Carlos Figuero's face flamed with answering enthusiasm. "True! Even I, Carlos, can do it! Give me your name to use, Silver, and the hills themselves will flock to your heels!"

A universal shout went up at that. "Turn us loose, Silver, and see what the men of the Hawk can do."

"We'll find two men to fight each other for every gun!"

AND SO began a saga which has become one of the legends of the Sierras Pequenas country. Varro's riders swarmed the countryside. Everywhere the small companies of the *Federalistas* were on Varro's side, ready to arrest any of the *Halcones* on sight, as outlaws. Yet, through that land swarming with enemies, a score of men rode, night and day, unscathed. Lean-faced, hard-bitten men, on lean and hard-bitten horses—ghost-like along the lonely trails, like thundering couriers of hope into the crowded settlements. "Up! Pass the word. El Diablo has met his match. Up! For your homes and your future. The Hawk needs men. Rouse out! The guns of justice wait for you. Will you march with Silver and be free men, or sit here like frightened hens while the coyotes raid?"

And from everywhere, from the lonely huts of goatherders deep in the hills, from humble farms and from the crews of great haciendas, from villages and towns, men came—simple men, grim-mouthed, who knew and hated the ways of El Diablo, who had resisted the blandishments of his recruiting bands, and who left fields and work behind them now, drawn by the magic of one name—Silver Trent!

By tens, and scores and hundreds, they drifted along the trail to the rendezvous, until the quota of a thousand could have been filled twice over, and only those who had brought their own rifles could be accepted.

So Silver Trent raised his army, while Esteban Varro schemed and drove men maniacally until he had made good his promises to his men, until the last one of the twenty-five hundred were equipped and fully armed....

THE VALLEY ran in a wide half-moon. On the north slope, half-concealed by the scattered rocks and brush, a slender line of men showed. There wouldn't have been more than five or six hundred of them, in two echelons. The broken rear had its two parts running out beyond the flanks of the front line. They were made up of about a hundred men each, on higher ground, so that they could fire over the heads of the front line, but more closely gathered, so that at need they could be easily shifted as a body to any part of the line.

The front line was widely spaced, with several yards between each soldier, so that its three hundred or more men occupied a wide, thinly held front.

Across the valley, some five hundred yards distance, was another line of men, also under cover, and containing perhaps half a thousand troops. Behind them, a long column filed through a gap in the hills, a column broke from time to time by mule-drawn field pieces and their caissons.

At one end of the valley, on a height, a group of men in the uniform of officers in the Mexican Federal Army stood watching the scene below.

Behind them, grinning and lounging at ease were a couple of companies of infantrymen, armed, but apparently filled with none of the tension of impending conflict.

Colonel Arturo Posillo y Jardenas, a lantern-jawed, able-looking soldier, in command of the detachment, stood side by side with his aide, El Capitan Fernando Igrazio.

The Colonel laughed contemptuously. "This bandit is mad," he announced. "When he attacked the head of their column and forced them to deploy, I expected something might come of it. A fairly bold and well executed maneuver. But this! Pah! With a line like that against a well-armed force of twenty-five hundred men. The Hawk might as well commit suicide and be done with it!"

The *Federalistas* had been marching with the Varro column, yet they were not of it. They had held a position well on one flank, so that they could be witnesses of anything which took place. That was in accordance with the money-oiled agreement the colonel had made with El Diablo. He and his men were to remain neutral, in any encounter, but would be allowed to be witnesses to the Varro victory.

OBVIOUSLY, IF Varro won, the *Federalistas* in the district would not be able to check the revolution. That was an understood thing. Yet technically, a battle between wealthy *hacien-*

dero's privately paid fighters and a collection of known bandits was none of the colonel's affair. Thus honor and expediency could both be satisfied. The colonel was a practical man, well able to hold his own amid the violent and changing politics of his native land.

His aide, Captain Igrazio, looked preoccupied. There was something like admiration in his intent gaze.

"Por Dios," he murmured by way of reply, "the man is mad enough, but there's a courage in him that one can't help liking." His chin lifted, motioning to where the figure of Silver Trent, mounted on a palomino horse, rode up and down between the echelons of his thinly held position.

"Mira!" the colonel exclaimed suddenly, "isn't that the priest of Sangre?"

He pointed toward a sturdy, be-cassocked figure, armed only with a crucifix, who also walked up and down between the lines, stopping from time to time to say a word to one of the "soldiers."

Igrazio nodded, smiling faintly: "The Fighting Padre of Sangre de Cristo. Sometimes I think that he is madder than the rest, but he, also, is brave."

"Dios, yes! Not one of them but is that. It makes a man almost wish—*Mira!* they start the attack."

It was so. The columns behind the Varro lines had deployed, field pieces on the slope and the foot soldiers moving forward to reinforce the front line. Behind these, held at the center, so that it could be thrown into any part of the line, were some two hundred and fifty mounted men, A long salvo of musketry rattled out from the line, the puffs of white from the rifles so closely spaced that, drifting upward, the smoke made one continuous layer. A scattering crackle of fire answered from the thin line of Trent men.

CHAPTER 13
THE MATE OF THE HAWK

THE VARRO advance began—an advance in the approved regulation manner, by squads that moved forward in turn, so that half the line was firing at the enemy while the other half was on its feet running forward.

It became apparent then, that the Varro lines were longer than that held by the Trent men. The ends overlapped. Now, these overlapping ends separated themselves still more, moving so as to encircle and flank the line of Silver's men.

The colonel threw up his hands. "It will be over in fifteen minutes," he pronounced. "I knew it would be if General Varro used the right tactics."

His aide glanced at him sideways, amused by the new respect shown in that "General" Varro.

The fire from the Trent line quickened, took on an almost desperate note. Yet there were men in that line who could shoot, for a surprising number of gaps showed in the advancing squads.

But there were not enough gaps. The advance continued. It threatened to sweep over the Trent lines like an engulfing wave.

"Pah!" The colonel spat. "This outlaw knows nothing of taking up a position. If he had to get himself in this fix, he might at least have put his lines up toward the crest, so that the enemy would have had a whole open slope to cross before they could get to him."

Then the Trent lines broke. A yell of terror went up from the men, and they raced rearward in a mad scramble.

A deep-throated shout of victory lifted from Varro's troops. A bugle blew a frantic, triumphant call to charge. The advance by squads ceased. The whole long line surged forward, bayonets glittering suddenly in the bright sunlight. Then the cavalry wheeled into action, charging straight through the center of their own lines, determined evidently to turn the mad retreat into a rout.

"As I said," the colonel snapped disgustedly, then his head canted to one side. "What's that?"

A queer stuttering sound had begun from somewhere.

"Gatling guns," Igrazio exclaimed excitedly. "There, on the flanks of the Trent line. See the smoke. He had them concealed there in brush all the time!"

"You are right! Will it stop them, though? I don't think so."

The stuttering sound stopped, picked up again.

"But they are hitting nothing!" the colonel raged. "Pah! It's enough to make a man sick!"

But something had gone wrong with the retreat. Halfway up the slope, the fleeing Trent men had stopped. Now they flung themselves down, as though by a prearranged agreement.

In the same moment, something happened to Varro's charging cavalry. The first horse, far in the lead, went down as though reaped by a scythe. The line, undeterred, galloped up to him. Then more horses went down. And more, and more! It was as though they had run into a fence which jutted out at a wide angle, with its corner to their center.

"What—what is happening?" the colonel stammered.

His aide slapped a thigh excitedly. "I see! I see!" he yelled. "They weren't shooting at them with the Gatling guns at all. They are shooting the guns on a certain line, toward each other, with the bullets meeting in and crossing one another in the center. It's like a barrier of steel—a death fence. It hurts nobody, until the advance runs into it, then they are mown down!"

He was fairly hopping about, in a frenzy of excitement. *"Mira! Mira! Hombre!"* The charge is broken! Mother of Mary! Look at those horses pile up. It is a shambles, a butcher shop. "And now the infantry hits it. Look! Look!"

THE COLONEL swore under his breath in an awed voice. Below him, the open floor of the valley was a pandemonium of screaming horses and cursing, howling men. Not half of the cavalry had gotten through that fence of bullet-death, and now these were stopped and shattered by sudden crashing fire from the Trent men in front of them. Then the first of the infantry, unaware of what it was that had broken the cavalry, had hit the crossing lines of Gatling gun bullets. It was as though a giant scythe keened through the air to cut them down.

The center struck it first, and melted away. Then caution hit in a sudden wave, running outward from the broken center along the flanks. The line stopped, dropped hastily earthward.

It was all that saved them. A few more steps would have brought them also against those crossed lines of almost continuous lead.

"Dios! I never saw anything like it," the colonel raved, light breaking in on him. "That retreat was a trick, to draw them on into that fence of death! This whole thing has been planned— superbly planned. He had his positions all arranged, his men rehearsed. Then he attacked Varro's columns, so as to make them deploy and fight on the ground he had chosen. Then that fake retreat, and…."

"Dios!" Igrazio yelled, dancing. *"Hombre!* Look! The flanks, the flanks!"

A column of ragged racing figures, four or five hundred of them, had debouched from a hidden ravine on the flank just below the hill on which the *Federalistas* stood, and were deploying in a line which enfiladed the Varro flank. Instantly, their rifles began to beat, crashing a death's tattoo.

On the other flank, a group of horsemen, some forty in all, appeared atop the ridge, and cantered straight down, so as to get on a line with the other Varro flank.

The Gatling guns had broken their hedge of fire now. Their bullets were going directly at the halted line now, by no means so deadly effective as they had been before, but chewing ragged gaps just the same.

"They're going to advance! They're going to charge!" El Capitan Igrazio was beside himself. "I go with them! I, Igrazio! For, by the saints, I am a warrior, too!

He jerked his revolver out of his holster with one hand, and his sword with the other, and flourishing them both wildly, began to run down the slope.

"Igrazio! Come back, you fool!" the colonel yelled after him. "The odds are still two to one. If Varro has any sense…."

BUT CAPTAIN FERNANDO IGRAZIO had the soldier's madness in his veins. He went plunging down the slope.

Below, the scene was frozen into one of those moments of immobility which come suddenly in the midst of the confusion and fury of a large-scale action. The Varro line, as though paralyzed, held its place. Nine-tenths of the men in it were directing their fire at the original Trent men in front of them, who were hard to hit, their second position having been well chosen in regard to cover.

The force on the flank was devoting itself to savage and intensive enfilade fire, and the group of horsemen, having got level with the other flank, had reined in and were firing coolly from the saddle.

About the only visible movement, apart from the puffs of gunsmoke, were some Varro horses, running, riderless, out of action. There were also jumping figures at one of the field guns, whose inaccurate fire had been silenced because their own line had been advancing too rapidly. But they now saw a chance to fire at the flanking detachment of Trent men.

Below, Silver had had the palomino horse shot from under him, and, to the relief of his men, stood behind the lines on foot rather than risk any more good horse-flesh. Padre Pete stood by his side, his round, pink face tranquil. But his eyes were snapping with excitement. There were four separate bullet holes in that tucked up cassock of his, but not a break in his apparently charmed flesh.

"Now, I think," Silver muttered. "Now if ever!"

He turned and signaled. A rider came galloping from the cover of the ridge behind him, leading two horses. Silver flung himself into the saddle of one of them and then flung his arms over his head, bringing them together in a great sweeping circle. The signal to advance!

The detachment of foot soldiers began on the flank first. In a short, close-knit line, they would run forward a few steps, pause and fire. The effect of their lead, concentrated in enfilade along the flank of the Varro line, was devastating. As always in enfilade fire, the bullets that went too high hit somebody else along the line, and Varro's men, facing front, were helpless to fire at their attackers, because they were lying down, and if they turned to shoot, their own men were in the way. And if they knelt or stood up, they were shot down by the Trent men on the slope.

A small section on the flank attempted to swing around to meet this enfilade attack, but when they got up to move they were mowed down by the Trent fire.

FROM BACK beyond the field guns, where Varro himself directed the battle, two mounted couriers shot forward.

Silver smiled grimly to himself. He knew that the only chance the Varro forces had now was to split into three sections, one continuing to face front and the other the sides—no matter how great the loss of life in executing the maneuver. Varro, of course, had seen that, and was sending down orders to his line commander.

He turned toward the mounted men on the other flank and

gave them the signal they were waiting for. Instantly, the group of horsemen surged forward.

A panic-stricken cry lifted from the Varro right flank as, guns slamming, the riders thundered down on them.

In the same instant, Silver's whistle shrilled and his great voice thundered, "Charge!" The line in front of him lifted to its feet with a yell and began to move straight down the slope.

From back of the field guns a black-cloaked figure, mounted on a magnificent stallion, flashed into view, racing toward the battle line. Varro! Belatedly, he had come himself to attempt to save the situation.

Silver's eyes gleamed. If he could get a chance at Varro.

The line was racing down the slope in front him. Out on the flank, where his riders were, Magpie Myer's high-pitched bubbling, blood-curdling yell sounded, followed by the savage, ringing battle cry of the Hawks. *"Hola, Los Halcones*! Hell's Hawks for Trent!"

Then they hit the flank of the line, rolling it up like a frayed edge of yarn. Already, the detachment of riflemen on the other flank had come to grips with the enemy, was chewing them up piecemeal.

Silver clapped spurs to his horse, jumped him down the slope. His great strides closed up the gap on his charging infantry, brought him out in the front of them before they hit the Varro line.

Then, suddenly, that line broke. A soldier, his face writhing in stark terror, tossed his rifle to the ground and turned, running.

"We're lost. Run!" His frantic screech cut through the hell's pandemonium of the gunfire.

It only needed that. Instantly, the line was broken in a dozen places as others took up his panic-stricken flight. Then, all at once, the whole Varro line was in wild retreat. Attacked from both sides and in front, their morale had broken completely.

A savage shout of triumph lifted from the Trent ranks. Merciless, they shot and bayoneted the men who fled them. In a moment, the field was a screaming shambles—a confused, out-spreading slaughter house.

Even now, the Trent forces were hopelessly outnumbered, and could have been defeated by soldiers who had the discipline and courage to stand and fight. But as it was, group after group of fleeing Varro men were overtaken and massacred by the enraged and victorious peasantry, who looked on them as dogs and traitors.

And through this confused and milling field of battle, Silver's riders slashed, criss-cross, back and forth, their deadly guns adding the final terror that insured the rout of the Varro forces.

But Silver Trent was no longer interested in the triumph of his forces. That black-cloaked figure which was Varro himself had pulled to a sliding, rearing halt when his line broke.

For a moment, his squawling voice lifted as he cursed his men and bade them stand. Then, seeing that the rout was hopeless, he raced to the rear, to save his own skin!

Silver Trent had hit the breaking Varro line like a thunderbolt. His hammering guns mowed down half a dozen men in his path, then be broke through, racing after Varro.

As though some instinct told him that his enemy was on his trail, Esteban Varro turned, slammed two futile shots at Silver and then bent low over his racing horse.

Then it happened. One of the Varro officers, who had been screaming at his men to stand, turned, his face contorted with rage, and leveled his gun at Silver, who was then not ten paces from him. Too late, Trent saw his danger. His right gun flipped up, blasting, just as the officer's Colt exploded.

His bullet took the Varro man squarely in the chest, bringing him down in his tracks, but in the same instant, Silver's horse went down, with the officer's slug in his brain.

Silver hit the ground hard, rolling. For a moment, the breath was knocked out of his big body. Then he was on his feet, surrounded by fleeing Varro soldiers.

A glance showed that Varro himself was already plunging into the canyon behind his field guns.

Silver cursed and yelled for a horse, but in that screaming, yelling, gun-blasting mêlée, even his great voice went unheeded. And he knew that Esteban Varro had slipped through his hands again.

Then, as abruptly as it had begun, it was over. Those of Varro's soldiers who had not been killed were standing in terror-stricken groups, with their hands over their heads, begging quarter.

Silver and his peasant army were left masters of the field, a field strewn not only with dead and wounded men but with the arms and ammunition which Esteban Varro had assembled with such difficulty, The revolution was broken—and with it, Esteban Varro's power!

Later, with his own Hawks accounted for and grouped behind him, Silver ironically, received the congratulations of El Colonel Arturo Posilla y Jardenas.

"Magnificent, Señor," the colonel was saying grandiloquently. "Mexico is your debtor. And I think that I can promise that our government will not forget you. When this news is heard, you and your men will no longer be outlaws!"

The shadow of a smile tugged at Silver's lips. "I'm afraid, Colonel…" he began, and then broke off to ask, "What will happen to Esteban Varro?"

The Colonel waved a violent arm; "Finished," he cried. "He is finished. His lands and all his property will be confiscated by the government. He—"

"You see—that's the trouble, Colonel," Silver cut in smoothly. "We are expecting to do a little confiscating on our own." He gestured toward a youngster who sat on a horse a little to one side. "There, for example, is Señor Bob Faraday, who is owed something like twenty thousand dollars by this El Diablo—not to speak of certain wounds for which he should be compensated."

Bob Faraday grinned at him, his eyes shining.

SILVER WAVED an arm toward his army, resting on their arms in front of him. "And there are my soldiers. They need some extra reward for this day's work. Esteban Varro has rich herds—rich possessions."

"Lastly," he turned, grinning at his men behind him, "there are my children there—my little cooing doves, whose feathers have been ruffled. Do they not deserve fine raiment? Rich food? Old wine? See! Two of them—only two, thanks to Pablo's saints!—have been wounded in this very fight. But all have risked their lives. The hawk's share of the loot should go to them, don't you think? Varro's fattest beeves, his finest gold and silver plate, his fastest horses…."

The colonel stirred uncomfortably. "I am afraid, Señor, that I cannot promise."

"No need to, *amigo*," Silver told him heartily. "We'll take care of all that ourselves! But I'm afraid that when we have finished, your government may be a little irritated. That ban of outlawry you so generously want to lift…." He shrugged his shoulders.

The Colonel found himself looking into a pair of gray eyes that had suddenly grown cold, a smile suddenly wolfish. He stammered. "Why, as to that, I—you…."

But Silver was no longer looking at him. A slender figure had moved into his field of vision—a figure clad in men's clothes, and dragging a rifle a little wearily in one hand. For an instant the breath stopped in his throat. Then, "Gracia!" he exclaimed. "What are you doing here?"

Color flooded the girl's face, and her eyes, drained by fatigue and emotion, came to life. "You didn't think you could keep me at home?" she said, defiantly. "You didn't think I'd let you go through it all alone?"

He was out of the saddle in one supple leap, and striding towards her. There was blood on the upper part of one arm.

"You're hurt!" he cried, in a voice which made the colonel jump, as though he were in some way guilty of this outrage.

Gratia shook her head. "Only a scratch of the skin," she said.

121

"I—I stayed behind the ridge, shooting from there, until the charge began. Then I joined in, and I—I couldn't make myself use the bayonet. A man—thrust at me, but—but somebody shot him and—and that's all."

Silver was gripping her shoulders, shaking her a little, almost savagely. "You were that near to death?" he asked in a voice that shook. "Gracia, don't you know that if you died I—I...."

"Yes, Silver?" A shameless glow had come into her eyes. She leaned toward him, her lips soft, parted.

Silver's fingers bit into her shoulders, while he fought the emotion that rocketed through him. Forgotten was his decision that she should share his dangers with him. This was too much. This had to stop.

He turned to the Mexican colonel and his voice had changed; "Colonel," he said, "If you still mean...." He stopped, torn. What of his men? What life would they find within the law? What life could be himself find?

It was as if Gracia had read his thoughts. "No!" she cried out passionately. "You'll make no deal with him! Have we fought, only to put ourselves in the hands of him and his crooked government? It's better for us to die than to sell our freedom. We're outlaws! Let's stay outlaws until the law is fit to live within!"

"We?" Silver looked almost dazed.

"Of course, 'we,'" Gracia snapped. "Do you think you can get rid of me now?"

Silver laughed suddenly. He swung on the open-mouthed Mexican officer, "Colonel," his voice rang out with exultation and pride, "I present you to the latest recruit of the Hawks, and another name for your roll of outlaws!"

The Colonel stared, voiceless, but not so the men behind Silver. The savage shout of acclaim they lifted left no doubt of their feelings.

But it was Doc Brimstone who raised the final yell—one that must have reached even Varro in his headlong flight.

"Let's get going for this loot, *amigos*," he bellowed. "Didn't Silver say wine? By the Britches of my Grandfather, I've got some drinkin' to do—to our new mistress, the Mate of the Hawk!"

POPULAR HERO PULPS AVAILABLE NOW:

THE SECRET 6
- ❏ #1: The Red Shadow — $13.95
- ❏ #2: House of Walking Corpses — $13.95
- ❏ #3: The Monster Murders — $13.95
- ❏ #4: The Golden Alligator — $13.95

OPERATOR 5
- ❏ #1: The Masked Invasion — $13.95
- ❏ #2: The Invisible Empire — $13.95
- ❏ #3: The Yellow Scourge — $13.95
- ❏ #4: The Melting Death — $13.95
- ❏ #5: Cavern of the Damned — $13.95
- ❏ #6: Master of Broken Men — $13.95
- ❏ #7: Invasion of the Dark Legions — $13.95
- ❏ #8: The Green Death Mists — $13.95
- ❏ #9: Legions of Starvation — $13.95
- ❏ #10: The Red Invader — $13.95
- ❏ #11: The League of War-Monsters — $13.95
- ❏ #12: The Army of the Dead — $13.95
- ❏ #13: March of the Flame Marauders — $13.95
- ❏ #14: Blood Reign of the Dictator — $13.95
- ❏ #15: Invasion of the Yellow Warlords — $13.95
- ❏ #16: Legions of the Death Master — $13.95
- ❏ #17: Hosts of the Flaming Death — $13.95
- ❏ #18: Invasion of the Crimson Death Cult — $13.95
- ❏ #19: Attack of the Blizzard Men — $13.95
- ❏ #20: Scourge of the Invisible Death — $13.95

DUSTY AYRES AND HIS BATTLE BIRDS
- ❏ #1: Black Lightning! — $13.95
- ❏ #2: Crimson Doom — $13.95
- ❏ #3: The Purple Tornado — $13.95
- ❏ #4: The Screaming Eye — $13.95
- ❏ #5: The Green Thunderbolt — $13.95
- ❏ #6: The Red Destroyer — $13.95
- ❏ #7: The White Death — $13.95
- ❏ #8: The Black Avenger — $13.95
- ❏ #9: The Silver Typhoon — $13.95
- ❏ #10: The Troposphere F-S — $13.95
- ❏ #11: The Blue Cyclone — $13.95
- ❏ #12: The Tesla Raiders — $13.95

MAVERICKS
- ❏ #1: Five Against the Law — $12.95
- ❏ #2: Mesquite Manhunters — $12.95
- ❏ #3: Bait for the Lobo Pack — $12.95
- ❏ #4: Doc Grimson's Outlaw Posse — $12.95
- ❏ #5: Charlie Parr's Gunsmoke Cure — $12.95

THE MYSTERIOUS WU FANG
- ❏ #1: The Case of the Six Coffins — $12.95
- ❏ #2: The Case of the Scarlet Feather — $12.95
- ❏ #3: The Case of the Yellow Mask — $12.95
- ❏ #4: The Case of the Suicide Tomb — $12.95
- ❏ #5: The Case of the Green Death — $12.95
- ❏ #6: The Case of the Black Lotus — $12.95
- ❏ #7: The Case of the Hidden Scourge — $12.95

Made in the USA
Coppell, TX
30 June 2021

58380904R00080